P9-CFV-749

The Turkey's Nest

By the Same Author

The Doubting Kind

The Turkey's Nest

Alison Prince

William Morrow and Company / New York / 1980

First published in Great Britain in 1979
by Methuen Children's Books Ltd.

Library of Congress Cataloging in Publication Data

Prince, Alison.
The turkey's nest.

Summary: Pregnant and unmarried, 17-year-old Kate leaves London to live with a distant relative on her farm in Suffolk while she decides about her future.
[1. Unmarried mothers—Fiction. 2. Farm life—Fiction.
3. England—Fiction] I. Title.
PZ7.P9358Tu [Fic] 79-28126
ISBN 0-688-22224-2
ISBN 0-688-32224-7 lib. bdg.

Printed in the United States of America.
1 2 3 4 5 6 7 8 9 10

1

"Kate!" shouted Mrs. Heath. "You done those eggs yet?"

"No!" Kate shouted back. "Can't Annie help?" The smell of hard-boiled eggs made her feel sick.

"No, Annie *can't* help," snapped Mrs. Heath. "We'll have no sandwiches ready otherwise." She mashed at a bowl of tuna fish, her apricot face creased with annoyance, then said, "Why are you so awkward?" Kate pulled the shell off another egg. Her stomach was heaving. "Give yourself airs, that's your trouble," went on Mrs. Heath. "It's this modern education. Makes you girls choosy."

"I'm not choosy," said Kate. "I just hate boiled eggs."

"Anything else you hate, while we're at it?" inquired Mrs. Heath sarcastically. "Just so as I know."

"Oh, yes, plenty." Kate suddenly felt reckless. "I hate the plastic cups and the awful stewed tea and the sloppy marge and those utterly repulsive meat pies. And—oh, never mind." And your ghastly green eye-shadow, she had almost said.

Mrs. Heath pursed her lips. "In that case," she said, "you'd better find yourself another job, Miss Carling. As from Saturday."

"With pleasure," said Kate briskly, but fighting down a secret dismay. Mrs. Heath looked at her for a minute or two, hand on hip, then remarked deliberately, "From what I hear, you'd have been leaving soon anyway."

Caught off guard, Kate blushed violently. Annie had promised not to tell anyone. And Annie must have been the one. Nobody else knew.

"You *have* been a silly girl, haven't you?" pursued Mrs. Heath. Kate wrestled with an eggshell, which pulled half the egg away with it, too shaken to find any response. Mrs. Heath came closer, exuding a powerful smell of synthetic flowers. "Listen, dear," she said. "I know we've had our little differences, but I can help you if you like. I know a very good address. No questions, and not too expensive."

"No, thanks," muttered Kate.

"Now don't be silly, dear–"

Kate flung the half-peeled egg back into the bowl and turned to face the manageress. "I don't want to talk about it," she said, trying to speak quietly because the other counter hands were doing their best to hear what was going on.

"Well, you'll have to talk about it before long, won't you?" remarked Mrs. Heath. "It's no use hoping it'll just go away, you know."

"I *know!*" said Kate, agonized. "But do shut up!—Everyone's listening."

"I'm not surprised," said Mrs. Heath, and turned away fastidiously.

Kate's fingers shook as she picked up the next egg. Wispy-haired Annie sidled up, looking rather frightened.

"Fine friend *you* are," said Kate.

"I didn't tell her," said Annie, shelling an egg neatly. "Honest I didn't."

"You must have told somebody."

"I didn't. Pauline guessed. It was when you said you'd gone off coffee. She said that's how she always knew she was pregnant, when the coffee tasted funny. And she's got three kids."

"Big deal. *I've* got the sack."

"Oh, no! I'm ever so sorry."

"I don't care. She can stuff her old job."

"What are you going to do then? Work in another snack bar?"

"I don't know," said Kate, bleakly. "I honestly don't know *what* I'm going to do."

When Kate came out of the Silver Snack Bar that evening, Laurie was waiting for her. He stood with his shoulders hunched against the February chill, his hands deep in his pockets and his coat collar turned up. Kate smiled. Trust Laurie to look dramatic, she thought. It wasn't *that* cold.

"Hello!" He smiled, thin-faced under the absurdly large, loudly checked cap.

"Hello. Been here long?"

"Quite a while. I had to take Barbara into hospital, and it didn't seem worth going home and coming out again, so I came straight here. Isn't it cold?"

"Feels warm to me after that stuffy hole," said Kate. "What did they say about Barbara?"

"Oh, the usual line. Going to try drugs and radiotherapy. The nurse said her piece about leukemia being terminal in most cases but not to look on the black side. Modern medical science is constantly improving, she said."

Kate nodded. There was nothing she could say about Barbara that hadn't already been said over and over again, and she felt very tired. She slipped her arm through Laurie's, and they set out toward the Underground station. It was rush hour and the pavements were crowded, so that the effort of avoiding people made conversation difficult. At the station she said, "I'm not coming with you tonight, Laurie."

"Oh, come on! We've got the place to ourselves, for once. I'll cook a nice meal and—"

"And we can sit and think about your wife in hospital. Great."

"I'm sorry. But it seems a bit tasteless."

"Does it? It doesn't to me, but then I'm not dishonest with myself—No, don't look like that, I didn't mean *you* were. Oh, blast, it's raining." Irritably he edged her around the corner into the thick warmth of the Underground station. "Look," he went on, "you know how things are about Barbara. If it hadn't been for the leukemia, she'd never have come back and you and I might have been married by now. I do *love* you, Katie."

"I know," said Kate sulkily, "but it's been a ghastly day, and I want to go home and wash my hair and think about things."

"And what am *I* supposed to do?" demanded Laurie.

"I don't *know*," said Kate.

"Well, ring me tomorrow. I'll be home all day, working on that pop-up book, boring thing. Who'd be a graphic designer?"

Kate did not smile. Laurie frowned. "Kate, what's the matter? You've been pretty casual lately. Is it something I've done?"

"No."

"Well, what is it then?"

"Nothing. I'm just tired." Kate badly wanted to get home to the quiet and solitude of her little bedroom. "See you tomorrow."

"Right." Laurie stepped back, snatched the ridiculous cap from his head, and swept her a courtly bow. "Anon, sweet one!" His thinning fair hair robbed the gesture of pomposity, and Kate laughed. Laurie could always make her laugh.

* * *

Standing wedged between other people in the crammed train, Kate tried to think. She would have to decide what to do. Her legs ached and she longed to sit down.

At Camden Town there was a changeover of passengers, and Kate managed to slip into an empty seat. The relief of not having to stand was wonderful. She stared at her reflection in the black window where ghostly pipes snaked along the walls of the tunnel outside. A small, rather chunky face under a thick mass of dark hair stared back at her. Short nose, greeny-gray eyes. Kate could see why Laurie called her Katie-cat. But she thought that in truth she resembled a pony rather than a cat. No feline creature could ever be so shaggy and disorganized as she was. Her father had been the same, an untidy, mop-headed man who never quite managed to look presentable. It had been one of the things that particularly annoyed her mother. But then Mum had a kind of effortless beauty, which filled Kate with envy and despair. She wondered vaguely whether her father was still alive, out in Australia. Surely there would have been some message if he had died.

Kate's reflection vanished as the train emerged from the London tunnels into the rainy daylight of the outer Barnet line. Good. The air seemed a bit less stale once out of the darkness. What a strange business this pregnancy was, she thought. It had changed everything so much. She had enjoyed being part of the London crowd, taken pleasure in having a quick answer for anyone who was cheeky at the snack bar. She was a London girl who could look after herself. But now she didn't belong anymore. She found crowds oppressive and longed for space and fresh air. London smelled so awful that she felt as if she would choke, and even the smells that she had liked had mysteriously turned sickening. Coffee, hot dogs, tar, and the general warm reek of humanity were all repulsive. She felt especially bad in the mornings when a shivering sweat of sickness made it impossible even to drink a cup of tea. Thank goodness she was always out of the house before Mum got up. Being an actress, she wasn't a very early riser.

Perhaps the row with Mrs. Heath was a good thing, Kate thought. It had forced her to realize that her secret couldn't remain secret much longer. Until now, nobody else had been concerned, but soon it would be other people's business. Laurie, Mum, doctors, Social Security. Ghastly. Why did one's private life have to be so public? Kate sighed. A lurch of dread intensified her perpetual queasiness. She would have to tell Mum, with no more delay and putting off. This very evening.

Outside the suburban houses flicked by, each identical to the other except for the tiny differences of colored paint, a store stork brooding over a plastic pond, a green plastic porch. Little boxes, little boxes . . . the song echoed in Kate's mind. What a way to live, she thought gloomily, like anonymous ants. But then what other way of life was there? She had no alternative to offer. All she had ever been certain of was what she *didn't* want. Sitting in a classroom, thinking on approved lines, joining teams. Living in Finchley, doing dull jobs. Being with mad, anarchic Laurie had been great fun until Barbara came back and spoiled it all. Poor thing, it wasn't her fault. But everything was in a muddle now. There was nothing to look forward to—not even a holiday now, not with the baby coming.

Holidays. Kate thought of Tuscany, where her mother's friend Sheila lived and where they had stayed for several summers. It was lovely there. Once again in her mind's eye she saw the sunbaked, stony, creamy-white earth where the vines grew behind the house. She had sat there for a long time once, watching a lizard perfectly still under the blue-spotched vine leaves. Remembering it, she was happy.

Walking up the road from the station, Kate tried to rehearse what she would say to her mother. "Mum, I'm going to have a baby." No, she couldn't. Not just baldly like that. "Mum, I want to tell you something." Her mother would look up, putting back the lock of pale red hair from her face with a graceful forefinger. "Do you, darling?" And then what?

There was a yellow Volkswagen parked outside the

house. Nigel's car. Kate's heart sank. She couldn't tell Mum with Nigel there. Relief mingled with her disappointment as she went through the side gate and opened the kitchen door.

"Hello, darling," said Kate's mother. She and Nigel were sitting on the bench seat by the table, on which stood empty teacups and a half-eaten packet of biscuits. "Had a nice day?"

"No," said Kate. "Have you?" She filled the kettle and switched it on.

"We've had a *lovely* day," declared Nancy Carling. "Haven't we, Nigel?"

"Don't be cryptic," Nigel rebuked her. "Kate, we've got something to tell you."

Kate almost laughed at this reversal of the conversation she had planned. "What's that, Nigel?"

"Your mother and I are going to get married," he announced.

Nancy put her arm around his neck and kissed his cheek. Strands of the pale red hair escaped from their Grecian knot and tumbled beautifully about her face. She smiled at her daughter. "Aren't you pleased, darling?"

"Yes," said Kate. "Of course I am." She had been so neatly upstaged that she felt emotionally winded.

Nigel was looking concerned, his big, doggy face furrowed with anxiety. "I hope you don't mind the thought of me as a stepfather," he said.

Nancy laughed. "Don't be absurd, Nigel," she said. "You've been one of the family for ages. It's just a matter of convenience, darling," she added to Kate. "Living the way we do, it's crazy to keep up two houses."

"I see," said Kate. "When's it going to be?"

Her mother looked at her a little uneasily. "Oh, we've no definite plans yet. Easter might be nice. But I'll put this house on the market straight away in case it takes a long time to sell."

"I see," said Kate again. The kettle boiled, switched itself off. "Do you want some more tea?"

Ignoring the question, her mother got up from the table and came across to Kate. "Darling, you don't *mind,* do you? I mean, you're seventeen now, and you and Laurie seemed so settled. Though I must admit, you've been here a lot more lately. But I didn't think you'd *mind.*"

"I don't. Of course I don't." Kate tried to smile reassuringly and then found, to her horror, that she was going to cry. "Teacups," she gulped, and ducked to get them out of the cupboard, hiding her face. Her mother was not deceived.

"Katie, darling, what is it?"

Kate shook her head blindly, groping for a handkerchief. But as her mother hugged her closely, the worry and secretiveness of the last four weeks overwhelmed her and she sobbed helplessly.

Nigel was looking deeply unhappy. He picked up his briefcase and said, "Look, you don't want me around just now. I'll see you tomorrow, Nancy."

"Please, Nigel, don't go!" pleaded Kate. "It's not because of you and Mum."

"What is it then?" demanded her mother rather crossly. "You've got yourself in a muddle of some sort, haven't you?"

Kate nodded, half smiling at the old East Anglian phrase, which covered all disasters. Wildly she tried to invent an alternative explanation. It was too awful to tell them the truth when they were so happy.

"Got the sack," she remembered, grateful for this comparatively trivial setback.

"Mustard in the custard?" asked Nigel, trying to cheer her up.

Kate shook her head. "Rude to Mrs. Heath."

Nancy Carling frowned impatiently. "You've been sacked from heaps of silly jobs," she said. "There's more to it than that, isn't there?"

"No," said Kate.

There was a pause. Nancy tidied a few strands of hair back into the tortoiseshell comb that held the loosely coiled bun in place. Nigel sat clutching his briefcase irresolutely and then said suddenly, "Are you going to have a baby?"

Kate stared at him, agonized. She only had to say yes, and yet even this was difficult. But the truth had to be told. She nodded, clenching her fists in her lap and looking down at them. She could not meet his eyes now. "Stupid, isn't it?"

"Oh, *Katie,*" said her mother. "You *silly* girl! Why ever didn't you tell me?"

But Kate could not answer.

"I'll make the tea," said Nigel.

After a while Kate felt a lot better. "I wanted to tell you before," she said, "but somehow I never could."

"The question is," said her mother, "what are we going to do?"

"How does Laurie feel about it?" asked Nigel.

"He doesn't know," said Kate. "Seems crazy, I suppose, but . . . oh, it's all so complicated."

"What you mean is," said Nancy, "Laurie's married."

"Yes," admitted Kate. "When did you guess?"

"I didn't. A chap at Television Center mentioned some graphics Laurie had done, and it just came out in conversation. Barbara."

Kate nodded.

"But he said they'd split up," continued Nancy, "so I wasn't too worried. When you told me Laurie wanted to marry you, I assumed there'd been a divorce."

"There would have been," agreed Kate, "but Barbara wrote to him out of the blue and said she'd got leukemia. The fellow she'd been living with shoved off—I suppose he couldn't bear it—and she was very pathetic and said Laurie was the only person she had ever really loved and could she come back? So he said yes. He's very sentimental really, once you get through his hard-boiled way of talking."

"When did all this happen?"

"About two months ago."

"Just when you—?"

"First thought I was pregnant. Yes."

Nancy raised her hands in a gesture of outrage, then let them fall in her lap. Nigel said indignantly, "Well, that's charming, isn't it? Is she still living there?"

"She was until today. She's gone into hospital for tests and therapy. That's why it's so complicated. I don't know what to think. In a way I loathed her for coming and spoiling everything, and yet I'm so sorry for her—I mean, she's probably going to die. How would *I* feel? And there's another thing. Since she's been back and I haven't seen so much of Laurie, I've found I can manage without him. I used to think I really needed him, but I don't. Not anymore."

"That," said Nancy, "seems a very good thing. I imagine you saw a different side to our Laurie when the going turned rough."

"In a way," Kate admitted. "It seemed a terrible strain on him. He couldn't talk about anything else. He said it interfered with his work and he couldn't sleep and couldn't ask anyone to the house. He got into an awful state. I worried about him for weeks, and then I thought, Well, there's nothing I can *do* about it. So I stopped worrying."

"I can see why you couldn't break the dread news," observed Nigel. "He'd have gone out of his mind."

"Yes," agreed Kate simply.

"But, darling," her mother protested, "you've got to *tell* him. Haven't you?"

"Yes," said Kate. "I'll tell him tomorrow."

There was no more to be said on that subject, and Nancy sat back from the table like a chairman winding up a debate as she came to the crux of the matter. "The main thing is," she said, "to get the medical side of things sorted out right away. Dr. Acot's pretty sensible, thank goodness. We'll go and see him first thing tomorrow—Oh, no, morning rehearsal. We'll go to evening surgery."

Kate took a deep breath. "Mum, I don't want to have an abortion."

"Katie!" For the first time, Nancy looked aghast. "Don't be absurd. You're only seventeen. You've got your whole life ahead of you!"

"I know," said Kate, "and what's it going to be? It's all very well for you, having a career and being beautiful and assuming that people can do what they like if they put their minds to it, but they can't. That's what I thought all the way through school, and so I made a total mess of it and never did any work and never took any exams and now what have I got? Nothing."

"If they wanted you to take their silly exams," said her mother, "they should have chased you up about it."

"Oh, they did," said Kate. "I just typed them a note on Laurie's typewriter saying I'd got glandular fever and signed it with your name."

"But I thought you were going to school—sometimes, at least."

"Of course I wasn't going to school," said Kate crossly. "I was around at Laurie's."

Nancy sighed. "I suppose this is the penalty for being a working mother."

"Whatever it is," said Kate, "I'm not having an abortion because of it. Why should I? So that I can go back to the Silver Snack Bar? If I'm a good girl and stay there for twenty years, I might get Mrs. Heath's job and boss people about over the boiled eggs. Oh, great!"

"But it's no reason for having a baby," argued her mother, losing her poise a little. "It's so irresponsible, making a new life just to see what it'll do for you!"

"No more irresponsible than destroying it!" said Kate hotly. "Don't you see, Mum, this is a sort of turning point. Looking ahead, I don't know what's going to happen or what it will be like, but looking back, there's nothing worth hanging on to. Having a baby will change everything, I suppose, but it can't make things any worse."

"Oh, can't it!" said Nancy darkly. "Just you see."

Nigel intervened. "I must say, I think Laurie is being quite unjustly left out of this. It's his baby, too, and it's his responsibility to look after it—and to look after you, too, Kate."

"But I don't—" Kate's protest was cut short by her mother's hoot of laughter.

"Nigel, you're such a Victorian! People don't have responsibilities nowadays. They just wait to see what happens and then cope as best they can."

"I don't care," insisted Nigel. "I'm perfectly prepared to look after you, if you'd let me, and I'll look after Kate, too, if Laurie shirks his duties."

"Oh, Nigel!" Kate was touched. "You *are* sweet! But I don't want to live with you and Mum. Not with a baby. We'd all mean well, but it just wouldn't work. We'd end up hating each other."

Nigel began to protest, but Nancy cut across him decisively. "Kate is perfectly right. We mustn't deceive ourselves because of emotional pressure." She leaned across the table and took Kate's hands. "You mustn't worry, darling. We'll think of something. What would you really *like* to do?"

The graceful, affectionate question filled Kate with despair. For the second time that day she answered, "I don't know." And the outlook seemed no less bleak than it had in the morning.

2

The next day Kate escaped from the Silver Snack Bar as soon as the lunchtime rush was over. She went into a phone box and dialed Laurie's number.

"Laurie Coppersmith." The name is what people want to hear, he had told Kate, not numbers.

"Laurie, it's me."

"Hello, you. Nice clean hair?"

"Hair?" For a moment Kate had forgotten what he meant; then she remembered his resentment of last night. "Oh, no, I never got around to hair washing after all. There was a lot to talk about."

"Such as?"

"To start with, Mum's going to marry Nigel."

"Nigel. That scruffy man who works at the BBC?"

"Yes."

"Must be crazy," said Laurie. "Getting married at their age. Years too late to have kids or anything."

"Is that what marriage is for?" asked Kate cautiously. "Having kids?"

"Yes, mostly. Give the little horrors a surname.

When I married Babs, I assumed I'd be a dad in no time. It didn't work out that way, but that's what I thought."

"Did you *want* children?" asked Kate with a sudden surge of hope.

Laurie laughed. "Good Lord, no! All my friends who've got them are up to the eyes in diapers and debts, and they can't go out without paying some nymphet to look after the brats, and when they *do* venture forth they can't talk about anything but teething rings. I dare say if Barbara had got pregnant straight away, I'd have accepted it quite cheerfully, but as things turned out it's a blessing she didn't. I mean, just fancy some jammy-fingered sniveler getting loose among my Letraset!"

"You could keep the studio door locked."

"What a horrid idea. Anyway, it's not just the studio. Think of spat-out biscuits ground into the carpet and bawling at three in the morning. What on earth are we talking about kids for, anyway? You're on the pill, thank God. Are you coming around this evening?"

"I don't think so."

"Katie-cat, do come!" he entreated. "It's ages since we've seen each other properly." But Kate felt as if she was leaving him behind, in the past.

"I got the sack yesterday," she said.

Laurie's response was prompt. "Good. Come and be my studio assistant. Starting now."

The rapid *pip-pip-pip* of the dialing tone sounded. Kate pushed in another coin and tried to gather her courage. She had rung up to tell Laurie about the baby, and she must do so. Or would it be easier to tell him when they were together? No. It wouldn't.

"Laurie? Still there?"

"Starting now," he repeated, unperturbed, "leave that silly snack bar and come around here."

"Got to work out me notice," said Kate in her snack-bar voice. "Else I won't get me cards, see?" She must tell him. Stop delaying.

"Blast yer cards," said Laurie.

There was a pause. Kate felt very breathless. "Laurie. . . ."

"What?"

"You know I'm on the pill. It can go wrong."

"No, it can't. Not if you keep taking it."

"If you forget."

"You're not going to forget, are you. Do stop chattering and come around here."

"I did forget."

"Doesn't matter this month, does it? Good Lord, since Barbara came back I've hardly had a chance to *talk* to you, let alone get you into bed! I still don't see why we couldn't have had a civilized *ménage à trois*. I mean, I did *tell* her I—"

"It wasn't this month."

"What wasn't?"

"Oh, Laurie," said Kate desperately, "do listen! It

was nearly three months ago, just before Barbara came back. You met me after work one Friday night with those cartoonist friends of yours, Keith and Betty. We went out for a meal then straight down to their place at Reigate for the weekend. And I didn't get a chance to go home for my pills. You hadn't told me we were going anywhere, you see. . . ." Her voice petered out. "Laurie?"

"So you're pregnant?" He sounded cold.

"Yes."

"You've taken your time about telling me. Who else knows?"

"Just Mum and Nigel. Oh, and some of the people at the snack bar."

Laurie's temper exploded. "Bloody marvelous! Tell everyone you work with but never mind about me! Just a casual phone call when you can be bothered to pop out, when you can spare the time from the vital task of buttering buns! And what's more"—fury almost choked him—"you trap me into saying at some length just how much I hate kids, then tell me I'm a father! Well, thanks very—"

Pip-pip-pip. The implacable tone cut across his tirade so effectively that Kate almost giggled. She was tempted to push the door open and leave the conversation unfinished. But that would only make things worse. Bravely she put another coin in the slot.

"Laurie?"

There was a long, breathing silence.

"Laurie?" said Kate again.

Laurie sighed heavily. "I'm sorry," he said. "I shouldn't have shouted at you. What a thing to tell me, though. All the worry about Barbara, and now I've got these blasted pop-up people screaming about their deadline—"

"I'm sorry," said Kate stiffly. "I didn't do it on purpose."

"We could have gone to fetch your blasted pills."

"We couldn't! Think what it was like. We'd had that super Greek meal, and Keith said on the spur of the moment, let's all go down to Reigate, and we jumped in his car and went. I couldn't say we'd got to go to Finchley first. It would have taken hours and ruined everything, you *know* it would!"

There was another pause. "Oh, *blast*," said Laurie wearily, and Kate could almost hear him throw his pencil down on the drawing board. "Just when I'm so broke. The BBC still owe me for those captions."

"What's that got to do with it?"

"Abortions cost money. If you want the job done decently, that is. Luckily I know a psychiatrist. He'll give you a ticket all right, no bother."

"I don't want an abortion."

"Oh, yes, you do," said Laurie ominously. "Now get off this phone, and I'll come and pick you up. I want to talk to you properly, with none of this *pip-pip*."

"Mrs. Heath'll have a fit if you come before six."

"To hell with Mrs. Heath," said Laurie.

When Kate arrived home that evening, the kitchen smelled appetizingly of chicken casserole. A batch of cherry buns stood on a wire tray beside a big bowl of stewed apples, and peeled potatoes waited in a saucepan of water to be cooked. It was all most unusual. Kate hung up her coat and went into the sitting room where her mother was studying a script. She laid the thick sheaf of paper aside as Kate came in and took off the glasses that she only wore when she was alone.

"Hello, darling. You're late."

"I've been talking to Laurie. I didn't know you were going to go mad in the kitchen. Smells marvelous."

"Impending grandmotherhood," said Nancy. "I suddenly felt all domestic." She was wearing a lacy shawl around her shoulders, but far from making her look grandmaternal it merely added to her studied radiance. "Did you tell him?"

Kate nodded. "He was furious."

"Men," said Nancy disparagingly. "What's *he* got to be furious about?"

Kate sat down and stretched her hands to the electric fire. "He thought it was the last straw." Then she laughed at the memory of the afternoon. "It was really rather funny. After I rang him up, he came around to the snack bar in a taxi, marched in, and said to Mrs. Heath, 'I wish to speak to Miss Carling on business.' She looked as if she'd swallowed a teaspoon, but she didn't say anything. And Laurie took me to that terribly old-fashioned hotel in Piccadilly and ordered afternoon tea. He said he wanted peace and quiet. But it was *so* quiet that we couldn't say a word, not with all those creepy waiters listening. So we sat there eating potted shrimps and fancy cakes, and I thought Laurie was going to explode."

"Wasn't it awfully expensive?" inquired Nancy.

"Oh, ruinous. Luckily a group of Americans came in demanding coffee and doughnuts, and they made so much noise and kept the waiters so busy that we could talk as much as we liked."

"But he doesn't want the baby?"

"No," said Kate. "He doesn't. To put it mildly." The latent sickness that threatened her all the time suddenly made her feel cold. There was a long silence.

Nancy turned over a page of her script but put it down again on her lap. She sat back on her chair and pulled the shawl more closely around her slim shoulders. "As you can imagine," she said, "I've been thinking about it all day. It's like an endless tape playing the same old monologue over and over again, full of blame and regret and 'if only.' But none of it's any use. The only thing I can say is that this is your home and it goes on being your home—and the baby's home, too. If it's not this actual house, that doesn't matter. After all, it's going to be my grandchild. I expect I'll be quite pleased, once I get used to the idea."

"Oh, Mum!" Kate was touched, but her mother held up a warning finger.

"There's just one thing. It's going to sound awfully tough, but I must say it so that we know where we stand. I'm *not* going to offer to bring the baby up. Lots of grannies do, but I don't feel I could cope with it."

"Of *course* not! I don't want *anyone* to look after my baby except me! Otherwise, there's no point in having it, is there?"

Nancy shook her head doubtfully. "I still think you're making an awful mistake. Someone else will *have* to look after the baby if you're going to earn enough money to support yourself. You won't want to live with me and Nigel all your life."

"I don't want to live with you and Nigel at all," said Kate. "You know that. What I'd really like to do is go somewhere else, away from here, so I could start afresh. There are homes for unmarried mothers, aren't there? Laurie has a psychiatrist friend who is connected with one in some way. They find you jobs and everything."

"Darling, you'd hate it!" said Nancy. "Look how you loathed school. You just aren't cut out for the communal life."

"Come to think of it," said Kate, "I've loathed almost everything for a long time now. So it doesn't matter much whether I like it or not. I just want to get away and give things a chance to change. Break the pattern."

"You can't have been all *that* miserable," protested Nancy. "You always seemed to have heaps of friends and lots to do."

Kate made no reply, and in a little while her mother said lightly, as if changing the subject, "You wouldn't fancy deepest rural England for a bit, would you?"

Kate shrugged. "Try anything."

"I was mulling over our friends and relatives today, wondering if any of them could offer a temporary refuge and I thought of Auntie Beth."

"Who's she?"

"Your father's eldest sister. She married a farmer called Jack Kennett, but he died some years ago."

"Oh, yes." Kate was vague. "I don't know much about Dad's family. Is that the place we went to once when I was little and I was frightened by the pig?"

"That's right. In Suffolk."

"Where's the old girl now then?"

"Still at the farm. It must be pretty run-down by now because she's on her own there. None of her children wanted to take up farming. Can't say I blame them."

"It sounds dreadful."

"It probably is. You said you didn't care whether you like it or not, but Auntie Beth might be a bit much. She certainly would be for me."

"No, wait a minute." Kate felt a flicker of interest. "Are you still in touch with this old bird?"

"She sends me a Christmas card each year. Usually it's just 'Love from Beth,' but this year she put a note in, saying I was welcome to come and stay for a bit if I felt like a change from acting. It was just after I'd done that 'Z Cars,' so I suppose she was curious about what I was like in real life. People do love meeting television faces. Or perhaps she really would welcome some company. 'It get a bit lonely here sometimes,' her note said. Beth's verbs can be a trifle quaint."

Kate stared at her mother. Irrationally she felt a complete conviction that this lunatic suggestion was going to become a fact. Trying to fight off her sense of fate, she said lightly, "It's worth a try, I suppose. Nothing lost if she says no. After all, she might hate the idea even more than I do."

"Very probably," agreed Nancy. "She's pretty odd."

"What sort of odd?"

"It's difficult to explain. Nothing wildly eccentric, but she seems completely indifferent to everything except the job in hand. She'll walk out in the middle of a conversation and feed the pigs. I'm sure she doesn't mean to be rude, but she always makes me feel as if I'm just a frivolous idiot."

"Sounds ghastly."

"She isn't, really. She's very kind at heart, but she *is* frightfully Suffolk. It's not like London, where talking is a kind of game. Suffolkers say exactly what they mean, or they don't say anything at all. Perhaps it's because town dwellers are packed so close together that they put up a hedge of talk between each other, and in the country where people live miles apart, they've got things to say that really matter when they *do* meet."

"M'm." Kate was not much interested in her mother's theorizing. She wanted to think about this new idea without being distracted by conversation. "Shall I put the potatoes on?"

"Yes, do, if you feel like eating."

"I'm ravenous. It's funny, but the sick feeling doesn't stop me being hungry. Not in the evenings, anyway."

Nancy nodded. "When I was expecting you, I ate like a horse every evening and was as sick as a dog in the morning. Rowley used to say it was a waste of food giving me anything."

Kate laughed. Her father *would* say that.

Setting the table in the kitchen, she tried to visualize some farm kitchen occupied by herself and mad Auntie Beth. Perhaps they would hack hunks of salt pork from a sooty ham dangling from the rafters and cook it over an open fire. Perhaps she would have to go and pull up turnips early in the morning while her aunt crouched over an evil pot of porridge, a rough sack thrown across her stooped shoulders. No, the farm couldn't be as primitive as all that. Not nowadays. But even if it was, it would be more of a laugh than a home. She dipped her finger in the potato water, tasted it, and put in a spoonful of salt. Did they have telephones in darkest Suffolk?

"Mum!" she called. "What did you say Aunt Beth's surname is?" Not hearing the reply, she went back into the sitting room.

"Kennett," repeated her mother. "Beth Kennett. Why?"

"If she's on the phone, we might give her a ring."

Nancy looked anxious. "Kate, dear, there's no hurry. For goodness' sake, don't rush headlong into the first crazy idea that crops up. I only meant it as a suggestion. I thought you'd recoil in horror."

"Yes," said Kate, "you're probably right." And she returned to the kitchen to make sure the potatoes weren't boiling over. She would need Wellington boots, she thought.

3

They stood in an awkward little group on the station platform, Kate and Nancy, Nigel—who had ferried them to Liverpool Street in the yellow Volkswagen—and Laurie.

Laurie wore a swampingly large khaki duffel coat because it was raining, and his nose was pink. His arrival had caused a slight stiffness among the others. He gave Kate a nosegay of violets, exquisitely surrounded by silver lace and glossy dark-green leaves. "They'll last all right until you get there," he said. "I packed their stems in wet cotton and bound them up with Saran. Great stuff, that." Then, a little furtively, he pressed a small packet into her hand. It was tightly bound with brown tape, but he deterred her from inspecting it closely. "Not now," he muttered. "Open it later, when you're alone." He gave her a look that beseeched her to say something befitting the high emotional temperature of the occasion, but Kate was paralyzed by this meeting of people to whom she was different things. Her mother's presence made it impossible to speak intimately to Laurie, and with Laurie there she could feel no ease between herself and her mother. Nancy Carling and Laurie both wore polite smiles, and from both there emanated the almost tangible wish that the other would drop dead.

Nigel, as the least involved member of the party, managed to make the most sensible statement. "If you don't like it, Kate, you can always come back."

Kate smiled at him. "Thanks, Nigel. I will. Like a shot."

Nancy adroitly managed to step in front of Laurie and obtain a moment's privacy with her daughter. "Darling, there's nothing I can say really. I'll write to you."

"Yes, please."

"Often. And, as Nigel says, come back at once if you're not happy. Just ring. We can come up to Suffolk and fetch you." She fished in her bag. "Here—something to read on the journey." She handed Kate a paperback book in an orange Penguin Books bag. "It'll amuse you. Keep you sane among the mud clots."

Laurie said rather loudly, "I shall have to go, I'm afraid. I've got a hell of a deadline this week." He gave a slight squawk as Nancy, stepping back, trod on his toe.

"Sorry," she said insincerely.

Laurie kissed Kate and hugged her to him closely. "I love you, Katie-cat," he whispered. He felt thin and wiry under the rough cloth of the duffel coat, and

Kate was suddenly overwhelmed with sadness. "Oh, Laurie," she murmured, "if only it was just you and me. If only nothing else mattered."

"Ah," he said, "if."

The guard blew his whistle, and Nigel opened the train door. "Better get in," he said.

Alarmed by the thought that the train might go without her, Kate scrambled aboard. When she had shut the door, opened the stiff window, and leaned out, she saw that Laurie had gone, striding away up the platform, pulling the hood of his duffel coat over his head. "Bye, Laurie!" she shouted. But he did not hear.

The big hand of the station clock ticked away the last minute before three o'clock. Nancy's gray eyes suddenly welled with tears, and she ducked her head so that her face was hidden under the white fur of her Russian hat.

"Oh, Mum," said Kate, beginning to feel her own eyes prickle, "please don't cry. I'll be all right, really."

Imperceptibly at first, the train was moving. The touching hands parted, and what had been a caress became a wave. Nigel put his arm around Nancy, and the two of them stood waving, receding from sight, dwarfed by the ribbed arches of the great station roof, until they were gone.

Kate closed the window. Carrying her armful of presents and her Zodiac-patterned burlap shoulder bag, she found the seat that Nigel had reserved for her. He had put her suitcase and her neatly folded parka on the rack above it. He really was the nicest boyfriend her mother had ever had, Kate thought. She sat down and put the violets, the package, and the book in its bag on the table in front of her. For the moment, she did not feel inclined to look at them.

The train gathered speed, rattling through the empty stations of Stratford and lavatory-tiled Maryland. Kate gazed exhaustedly at the dirty cubic landscape of East London, feeling simultaneously lost and yet glad to be alone. It was barely a week since the phone call to Auntie Beth, a week of sorting and packing and saying good-bye and endless talking. Laurie, in particular, had gone on and on. Even after he gave up trying to persuade her to have an abortion, he had turned to the hope of adoption. "For God's sake," he kept saying, "you're so *young*. I'm ten years older than you, and *I* feel young. But you're going to turn yourself into a wrinkly handed old diaper washer —at seventeen!"

Kate had said snappily, "You're so worried about your image, Laurie. It must be a sign of insecurity."

A tremendous quarrel had ensued, and Laurie's huffiness had lasted until last night's farewell dinner, which he had cooked with the aid of *Larousse Gastronomique*. Then he had suddenly said, "If you *must* have this kid, I suppose you may as well call yourself Mrs. Coppersmith."

Tactlessly Kate had returned, "What's the matter with Miss Carling?"

Then he had been angry again. "I suppose my name's not good enough for you?"

But, for the present at least, all that was over. Kate turned her attention to the things on the table. She smiled at the almost embarrassing perfection of the nosegay. It was so like Laurie to go one better than a mere flower shop could do. She buried her nose in the dusky purple flowers but found to her surprise that they had no smell. She picked up the tightly wrapped package and shook it. Nothing rattled. Why had he told her to open it when she was alone? Curiosity overcame her. Picking at the tape with her fingernails, she started to tear off shreds of brown paper, stuffing them into the inadequate little bin under the window. The package was bandaged and cross-bandaged with all the perverse intricacy of a Pass-the-Parcel package at a party game. The last of the brown paper fell away and revealed a bulging white envelope, doubled in half. Released from its bindings, it sprang open, and Kate saw to her astonishment that it was packed full of crisp new five-pound notes. Turning it over, she found inscribed on the other side of the envelope in Laurie's graceful writing, "In case you change your mind. I love you, and you alone."

Kate leaned her head back against the seat, feeling rather breathless. What an amazing thing to do! Such generosity was astonishing—and infuriating, too. He was still trying to make her have an abortion. Furtively Kate counted the notes in the envelope. Three hundred pounds. He didn't do things by halves.

Outside the London suburbs were giving way to the sooty countryside of Essex. Lakes of water lay in the fields where grazing cattle stoically turned their backs to the east wind. If that's the country, Kate thought, I'm not going to like it. She put Laurie's money away carefully and then slipped her mother's book out of its bag onto the table. *Cold Comfort Farm* by Stella Gibbons. On the flyleaf Nancy had written, "Forewarned is forearmed! Wishing you all fortitude. My love. M." The publishers' blurb described the book as "the classic satire of country life." Kate grinned. Good old Mum! Even in moments of crisis, she never lost her poise. What was it she had said about Auntie Beth? "Her verbs can be a trifle quaint."

Kate felt a lurch of uncertainty as she realized that she would meet Auntie Beth, verbs and all, in a little over an hour's time. What a crazy thing this was, rushing off to live with some primitive woman who didn't even speak the Queen's English! For a moment she wished she had never embarked on the scheme. But the reasons were still there. Mum wasn't really a domesticated person; she was much more interested in her career than she was in housekeeping. Even when Kate had been quite small, when her father had first left home, her mother had treated her as a kind of sister rather than as a child. Kate had enjoyed her freedom, but the teachers at the school that she was supposed to attend regarded her with almost universal despair. When she left, Mr. Hepworth the art master was the only one to express regret. "You could have done something, Kate," he said gloomily. "But then art schools are so God-awful, talented people shouldn't go to them. We are enmeshed in mediocrity." Mr. Hepworth was always gloomy.

The train was running through the wide Essex marshes, where inlets of seawater wound in convoluted patterns between the mud flats. Seagulls wheeled against the gray sky or stood hunched on the mud. Nothing grew except long, harsh-looking grass. Kate stared, secretly afraid. Was Auntie Beth's Willow Farm going to be in a landscape like this? And what sort of people could inhabit such a place? They must surely be hard and bitter, toughened by years of endurance to show no weakness or sympathy.

Oh, God, said Kate to herself, what a fool I am. She huddled deep into her corner seat and tucked one leg under the other as if the warmth of the train's heater might be the last comfort she would know. She glanced at the book her mother had given her, but did not pick it up. *Cold Comfort Farm.* The title was too ironic to be funny. She stared out into the fading daylight as the train hurtled northward.

4

It was nearly dark when the train arrived at Coptoft Magna station. Kate got out, encumbered by suitcase, bag, and violets. The half-dozen or so regular travelers had occupied the carriage that landed opposite the station door and had rapidly disappeared, but Kate was at the far end of the wooden platform. It stood high up on an embankment, and when the train pulled out, taking with it the last connection with London, Kate found herself completely alone. There was nothing to be seen above the high fence except the vast sweep of darkening sky and the dwindling tail-lights of the train.

Then, hurrying toward her along the platform, Kate saw a figure that, she knew at once, must be Auntie Beth. Stockily built, she wore a woolly hat, a parka with three inches of blue nylon smock sticking out under it, trousers, and, Kate noticed with sinking heart, Wellington boots.

"*There* you are," she said, as if Kate had perversely

chosen to get out in the wrong place. She nodded at Kate's suitcase. "That all you've got?"

"Yes," said Kate, "but it's awfully heavy. Could we get a porter or something?"

"Expect I can manage," said her aunt. She picked up the suitcase with no sign of effort and set out beside Kate toward the station exit. Her face was red and raw-looking, with a shapeless nose, small eyes, and slightly protruding teeth. Strands of gray hair escaped from under the woolly hat. She was, Kate thought, the ugliest woman she had ever seen. She glanced at Kate's violets and said, "Hothouse?"

"I suppose they must be," said Kate. "Laurie gave them to me." She ought to give some explanation of who Laurie was, but it seemed very difficult. She did not want to go into detailed explanations for somebody she had only just met. An awkward silence lasted while they went through the tiny waiting room and down a flight of steps to the station yard. A large green van stood outside the parcels office where an official notice proclaimed, *No Parking*. Used to London traffic control, Kate said, "You'll get a ticket!"

Her aunt glanced disparagingly at the notice. "That's only when the post come," she said. "In you get." Then she dumped Kate's suitcase in the back and climbed into the driver's seat. Without speaking, she started the engine, switched on the headlights, and drove the van out of the yard.

"Is it far?" asked Kate.

"Not very," said her aunt. After a while she added, "I left a bit of food ready."

"Lovely," said Kate. "I'm ravenous." She had felt too sick to eat anything this morning, and the train buffet had looked so much like the Silver Snack Bar that she had gone straight back to her seat. Determined to keep the conversation going, she said, "You live on a farm, don't you?"

"That's right."

"It must be a busy life."

"There's plenty to do," agreed her aunt.

Kate gave up. She did not feel that her aunt was being unfriendly; she simply did not seem to have anything to say. But suddenly she remarked, "I left a cow calving. That's why I'm dressed a bit untidy."

"Oh, I *am* sorry. What an awful time for me to arrive. Will she be all right?"

"Should be. It's not like a heifer."

"What's the difference?"

"A good old cow that's done it before, she know what to expect. With a heifer it's all new, and she might get into a panic."

Kate smiled ruefully. "I think I know how she feels," she said.

"No excuse for humans," said her aunt firmly. "They can understand what they're told."

Feeling reproved, Kate lapsed into silence. Her aunt

turned off the road down a narrow track. It was dark now, and the van's headlights showed tall hedges on either side. Kate began to feel like Alice falling down the rabbit hole, for the track sloped downward quite sharply and, intensifying the fantasy, rabbits rushed away from the oncoming van, their white tails bobbing erratically.

Suddenly the hedges gave way to open space. Kate realized that they had come down from a road running along a ridge and that the farm lay along the side of a valley.

"There must be a lovely view in daylight," she said.

"You can see a fair way," agreed her aunt. The van rattled over a bridge with low stone parapets and came to a halt in a yard surrounded on three sides by buildings. Auntie Beth switched off the engine and got out, leaving the door open.

"I'll just have a look at that cow," she said.

Kate shivered in the icy air that poured into the van. It was very quiet, and the clatter of a bolt being shot back on one of the nearby buildings startled her. A light was switched on. Like a moth, Kate got out of the van and went toward it. Anything was better than sitting alone in the cold and the dark. The building was an old-fashioned cow shed with a stable door, which Kate leaned over. A cow was licking a wet calf that lay sprawled in the straw. She gave a deep call, so low that it was hardly more than a rattle in her throat. The calf moved convulsively and waved its head about, then flopped back into the straw. "Is it all right?" whispered Kate anxiously.

"It's fine," said her aunt. "Only been born a few minutes. Good girl, Dora. Clever girl you are." She knelt down beside the calf and rubbed it vigorously with a twist of straw while the cow continued to lick it. In a little while the calf made a great effort and managed to straighten its hind legs so that it stood comically with its rear end in the air and its head still down in the straw. Kate laughed and the cow jumped at the unfamiliar sound. "Ssh!" said Auntie Beth sharply.

"Sorry," murmured Kate.

The calf stood for a moment on all four legs, then collapsed into the straw, but after several efforts it made a successful attempt to get up. Finding the swollen udder, he poked blindly at a teat and soon, with some help from Auntie Beth, was sucking strongly.

"He looks much better now," whispered Kate.

"Yes," agreed her aunt. "He'll do. Now come along into the house." Leading the way across the yard, she added, "I hope you haven't got cold, standing there."

"Not a bit," lied Kate. "I suppose you have to expect things like that on a farm."

"That's right."

"And anyway," Kate went on, "I'd never seen anything like that before." This time she spoke the simple truth. "I thought it was lovely."

The door opened into a small, square hall with a brick floor. It was oddly furnished with several piles of crates and boxes, a filing cabinet, and an immense mahogany desk, which was stacked with trays of brown eggs. Coats and smocks hung on the wall, and a shotgun stood in the corner beside a mop, an umbrella, and a broom. Beside the desk was a velvet-seated Victorian swivel chair.

"This is the office," said Auntie Beth. She kicked off her Wellingtons and pushed her feet into a dilapidated pair of slippers. Then, carrying her boots, she opened the farther door into the kitchen.

"What a huge room!" said Kate. The kitchen was about eight times the size of the one in Finchley. There were windows in the walls on either side, indicating that the room must occupy the full width of the house. Armchairs and a big, comfortable settee stood around the big, coal-burning Aga stove, and there was still plenty of room for a huge pine table and half a dozen wooden chairs. And, Kate noticed with relief, there were lots of modern conveniences: fridge, washing machine, spin drier, deep freeze. At least the house wasn't primitive, Kate thought. Her aunt went over to the Aga, where a black-and-white dog lay quietly, nose on paws.

"Move over, Glyn," she said. "Make room for my boots." And to Kate, she added, "That make a lot of difference, warm boots in the morning." The dog gave Kate's hand a cursory lick, then lay down again. "Getting old," said Auntie Beth. "Like me. Take your coat off. You can hang it in the office."

Kate did as she was told. When she came back, her aunt had put knives and forks at one end of the table and was getting a foil-covered dish out of the Aga. "There's some baked spuds with it," she said. "I didn't think you'd want to wait while I cooked proper vegetables."

"It smells lovely," said Kate. Under the foil was a light suet crust, which gushed delicious brown gravy when cut. "M'm!" said Kate, tasting. "It *is* lovely!"

"Nice to have someone to cook for," said her aunt.

Cold plums and cream followed, and then the table was quickly cleared and Kate found herself sitting by the fire with a cup of coffee. Stirring, she looked at her aunt thoughtfully. Without the woolly hat her butcher-red face looked younger. Her gray hair was tied back with a piece of thin ribbon in a style that could not be called a ponytail because it was not a style at all, but simply a practical means of keeping the hair out of the way. Her thick sweater gave her a bulky appearance, and yet her neck and wrists were thin, lending an impression of frailty that consorted oddly with her robust capability. She looked up.

"I reckon you think you've come to a funny place," she said.

Kate blushed. "Not a bit," she protested politely. "It's a beautiful old house."

But this was not what her aunt had meant. "You'll have to see how you get on. Can you drive?"

"No," said Kate. "There didn't seem much need for it in London. There's the Underground, you see, and buses." And, she added silently, driving was far too expensive even to think about.

"Oh. When's the babe due?"

"In August."

"Six months. You'll no sooner have learned to drive than you'll be off again. Well, I hope you don't mind your own company. I can't be running into Hadham every day or so."

Kate took a deep breath. "Auntie Beth, I don't want to be any bother to you at all. I didn't come here for that."

"I think you best call me Beth," said her aunt. "You're too big to call people Auntie. And you don't want to worry about bothering me. I thought about that when your mother rang up, before I said you could come. I've got time enough for you, my dear." Her smile was unexpectedly sweet and engaging, and Kate was disarmed by her direct honesty.

"All the same, I don't want to be a nuisance. Perhaps I might even help. There must be lots to do."

"It take a time to get into the way of it," said Beth cautiously. She thought for a bit, then added, "Of course, farming may run in the family."

"Yes," agreed Kate cheerfully. "After all, I am a farmer's niece."

"A farmer's daughter," Beth corrected. "Your father's farming, isn't he, out in Australia?"

"*Is* he? Are you still in touch with him?" Kate was excited. "Mum hasn't heard from him for years. But then she *is* awful about answering letters."

"There's a lot of people I write to," said Beth. "That make something to do in the winter evenings."

"Fancy Dad farming," mused Kate. Then she laughed. "I can't imagine Mum as a farmer's wife!"

"That was the trouble, wasn't it?" said Beth. "Or half of it, anyway."

"Oh." Kate remembered something. "Mum gave me a letter for you. It's got a check in it." She was slightly embarrassed, but Beth was matter-of-fact.

"Thank you. I'll be going into the bank in Hadham tomorrow, so I can deposit it then. Have you found out about maternity benefits and that sort of thing?"

"No," confessed Kate.

"Then we'll do that tomorrow as well. Now you'll be tired after your journey, I expect. I'll bring your case in and look at that cow." She got up and went out. The slowly ticking grandfather clock said ten past nine. Kate eyed it in disbelief. Ten past nine, if the clock was right, was an absurdly early hour to go to bed. She looked at her watch. Ten past nine. Apart from the slow, heavy ticking and a faint sound of breathing from the sleeping dog, the silence was intense. Kate washed up the coffee cups and thought about Beth, living alone in this place with pitch darkness outside and no company except for an old dog and a ticking clock. Most people would find such solitude frightening.

Beth came in with Kate's case and carried it straight across to the staircase, which led up from the corner of the room. There she turned and said, "Did you want any cocoa or anything?"

"No, thank you," said Kate. "I'm still full of supper."

"That's what I thought," said her aunt.

Kate followed her up the winding stairs. "Is the cow all right?" she inquired.

"Fine. Nice little calf she's got. Good back on him."

"Have you got a lot of cows?"

"Twenty-eight. Suckler herd. And I always have one as a house cow. Here's your room." She opened a door by its latch and switched on the light.

"Oh, it's *sweet*!" said Kate, surprised as well as delighted.

The room was small and mostly white, though its uneven walls were papered with faint rosebuds. The curtains, too, were flowered, but the furniture was all white-painted and the bed had a pale gray eiderdown and a white candlewick bedspread.

"I turned your electric blanket on," said her aunt,

"so that'll be nice and warm. The bathroom's next door."

"Thank you," said Kate. "That's marvelous."

"There're a good many books if you want something to read," said Beth, nodding at the shelf. "I like a read before I go to sleep."

"So do I," agreed Kate, "but Mum gave me a book. It's called *Cold Comfort Farm.*" She gave Beth a slightly uneasy glance, wondering if she would find this ironic.

"I expect she thought that was suitable," her aunt said gravely. But her smile contained a hint of malice, and Kate giggled. Her aunt was, as her mother had said, an odd woman, but there was something about her that Kate instinctively warmed to.

"Thanks for everything," she said.

"That's all right," said Beth. "Good night."

"Good night," said Kate.

The bed was, indeed, beautifully warm. Kate felt a comforting sense of luxury as she cuddled between the fresh-smelling sheets, but there was, too, the shivery sense of half dread that had become familiar since she knew she was pregnant. Her breasts tingled uncomfortably, and although there was no difference yet in her visible shape, she could feel with her hand the small swelling that was starting to invade her body. It was something she was constantly aware of, although it seemed more remote during the day, when other things claimed her attention. But at this solitary, private time of going to bed she felt as if she were meeting herself again after a day's interruption. Here we are again, she thought sleepily in the ludicrous music-hall phrase, happy as can be. She reached for her mother's book and began to read.

5

Kate woke the next morning to wintry sunshine filtering through the flowered curtains. It must be late. Warm and lazy, she lay still, gazing at the unfamiliar room. The furniture, she thought with faint amusement, was the sort of stuff people bought from junk shops in London to strip down to the original pine and resell at great profit. But nobody here would dream of disturbing the layers of white paint. Laurie's nosegay of violets stood in a glass of water on the marble-topped washstand. So Beth must have been in already this morning.

A door slammed below, and Kate heard footsteps coming up the stairs. She pushed the bedclothes back and sat up in guilty haste, forgetting the nausea that lay in wait. Beth tapped at the door and came in with a tray. "Good morning," she said. "And how are you?" She put the tray down and pulled the curtains back. Frosty sunlight streamed in.

"I'm fine," said Kate, keeping very still. She felt desperately sick.

"You got up too quick," said her aunt, looking at Kate's white face. "Gave yourself a dizzy turn. Try a biscuit." She handed Kate a plate of thin Morning Coffee biscuits from the tray. Kate took one and nibbled it dubiously while her aunt sat down on a wicker chair, stirring a cup of tea.

"What's the time?" asked Kate.

"Just after nine," said Beth. "I always have a bit of breakfast about now, when I've finished the milking and feeding."

"I didn't mean to sleep so long," Kate said apologetically. "I got up all right when I worked at the snack bar."

"What time did you start there?"

"Eight o'clock."

"Did you like it?"

"No, it was awful. I was always getting in a row for putting too much in the sandwiches. You had to put it just around the edges so it showed."

"That's not very honest," said her aunt. "Couldn't you find anything nicer to do?"

Kate shrugged. "I tried office work. That's boring. I'd rather do something practical."

"I couldn't be doing with an office," agreed her aunt. "Do you want your tea now?"

"Yes, please." To Kate's surprise, the sickness had subsided quite a lot.

"There's a letter for you," said Beth, handing Kate an envelope. "Pretty writing."

"It's from Laurie," said Kate. "He's my—I mean, he's—"

"The babe's dad?" supplied Beth.

"Yes," said Kate gratefully, opening the envelope. The graceful calligraphy was restrained to a small area in the center of the white page, like a sonnet in a poetry book.

"He don't care how much paper cost then," said her aunt, with a disparaging glance at the letter. Kate smiled and began to read.

Darling girl,
It is dawn as I write. By the time you read this I will have seen you once again to say a sterile last good-bye, but the loneliness of now reminds me ceaselessly that you have gone.

My love, I wish that I was more to you.
You have my unborn child as part of you
Yet I, the maker of this cherished life,
Remain alone. And I have been alone
So much these last few weeks, and felt you slip
Away, alone yourself, and shutting me
Outside. Beloved girl, remember me.

Mundanely, you will by now have explored the contents of my gift to you. I had to take a chap from Accounts out to lunch last week to hurry that check up, but it's worth it to know that you can keep your options open a little longer. As my halting pentameters try to say, I think of you constantly and of the baby you want so much, though I am still sure that its birth would be a tragic error. I want so much to pick up the threads of our life together, and yet I have a sense of doomed finality and feel that wurzel grubbing will claim you forever.

Good-bye, my love.

In limbo.

L.

Kate folded the letter between her fingers, frowning. She felt half inclined to cry, and yet in some ghastly way it was almost laughable.

"I really did love Laurie," she said, as if defending herself. "But now the more I think about it the more I'm not sure. It's awful."

"I'm going into Hadham this morning," said Beth, as if Kate had not spoken. "You'll want to get fixed up at the hospital. My doctor does the prenatal clinic, so you'll be all right."

"Yes, of course," said Kate, stuffing the letter back into its envelope. "Sorry if I'm keeping you waiting." Her tea was cooler now, and she drank it quickly.

"Don't rush," said Beth. But Kate handed her the empty cup and scrambled out of bed. "That was lovely," she said. "Thank you very much."

Her aunt piled the things onto the tray. "If you're ready in half an hour," she said, "we'll go. Are you feeling better?"

"Much better," said Kate. "Thank you."

"No need to keep thanking me," said Beth, and went out.

In the van on the way to Hadham, Beth suddenly asked, "What are you going to call yourself? Mrs. Something?"

"Laurie said I could be Mrs. Coppersmith," said Kate. "That's his name. And he did want to marry me. I mean, he still does, only he can't just yet." She thought about Barbara but decided not to go into all that. "What do *you* think?"

"Nothing to do with me," said Beth firmly. "You make up your own mind, long as I know what to call you if people come."

"I think I'll stick to my own name," said Kate after some thought. "After all, I do *want* the baby, so there's no point in pretending to be someone else."

"That's all right then," said her aunt.

They drove on in silence for some time. Kate, gazing out the window, felt as if she was seeing the countryside for the first time. Living here was not like going out for a Sunday drive. These fields and farms and patches of woodland were going to be her neighborhood. "I thought Suffolk was flat," she said.

"Parts of it are," said Beth. "This bit's quite humpy."

The flowing lines of the plowed land swung down into a hollow and up the far side, disappearing over the shoulder of the hill. "It's like a tiger," said Kate, fascinated.

"What is?"

"The stripes on the earth. Like a tiger lying down. It's the way the stripes sort of follow the shape."

Kate stopped, feeling that she had been far too fanciful. But her aunt nodded appreciatively. "I like to see a nice bit of plowing," she said. After a while she asked, "Have you lived in the country before?"

"No," said Kate. "When I was small and Dad was still with us, we lived in Hampstead. We used to take the dog for walks on the Heath. Mum got rid of the dog after the divorce. She was doing a lot of television work then, so she couldn't look after him. And I was at school all day. That's what I minded most about it really—Bruce going. And after that we moved to Finchley. Mum didn't seem to be getting so much work, and it was cheaper."

"Pretty name, Finchley," said Beth. "Is that in the country?"

"Lord, no," said Kate. "I suppose it must have been a village donkey's years ago, but it's all shops and houses now. Part of London."

"So you've always lived in a town."

"Yes. The only country place I know is in Italy. Mum's got a friend there, and we've gone for holidays sometimes. I loved it. You could go out from the back of the house, up a steep path between the vineyards until you got to the open meadows right up on the mountains. There were cows around in the summer, and the man who looked after them lived in a little hut. He had some chickens in a pen, and I used to feed them grass because it looked so bare. They gobbled it up, but I always wondered afterward if it did them any harm."

"No, chickens love a bit of green," said Beth. "You won't have hurt them."

Feeling absurdly reassured, Kate gazed contentedly at the passing landscape until they reached a garage, then a bungalow, then houses on both sides of the road. They had arrived in Hadham.

"Dr. McTaggart is the big white chief," said the young man pleasantly. "You'll be seeing him at the prenatal clinic on Thursday, I expect. I'm Dr. Marsh. We can do all your routine bits and pieces today and fill in a form or two."

"OK," said Kate. Dr. Marsh was plump and cheerful, wearing a tweed suit under his white coat. He took Kate's blood pressure and asked a lot of medical questions, noting down the answers. Then he sat back in his chair, twiddling a pen between his fingers.

"Now, Kate," he said, "I'm sure you've thought of all this, but you do know what you're letting yourself in for, don't you?"

Kate stared at him suspiciously. Was he going to lecture her on being irresponsible? It was none of his business.

"I'm not going to insult you by implying that you are taking this pregnancy lightly," he continued, "because I don't think you are that sort of person. But every time I see a woman have a baby it strikes me afresh that it's an overwhelming thing. Drastic. Nobody is ever quite the same again."

"So?" inquired Kate defensively. He smiled.

"So all I want to say is, the more you give in to what's happening to you and cooperate with it, the better it seems to be. Sometimes young, fit people like you feel that it's something that doesn't touch them essentially, that it's something they can do with one hand tied behind their back, so to speak. And it can come as a terrible shock that it's so powerful."

"But I *want* the baby," said Kate. "I keep telling people, it's the most important thing that's ever happened to me. The *only* important thing."

Dr. Marsh's smile widened to a boyish grin. "That's great!" he said. "That's the ideal attitude. It's the women who try to preserve a part of themselves untouched who really suffer, because they can't. Pregnancy is a massive take-over bid." He looked thoughtful and added, "Have people been at you to have an abortion?"

"Yes," said Kate.

He shook his head. "It's still technically possible, but I really wouldn't advise—"

"Don't worry," interrupted Kate. "If I'd wanted an abortion, I'd have had one by now. It's not that difficult. Not in London."

"Fair enough," said Dr. Marsh, scribbling a note.

"Now take this to the prenatal clinic on Thursday afternoon. The social worker there will tell you all about your benefits, and you'll meet Dr. McTaggart. Oh, and you'll need a urine specimen. All right?"

"Fine," said Kate.

That night she wrote to her mother:

Dear Mum,
It seems ages since I left you and Nigel at the station. What a horrid moment it was when the train started to move—I almost wanted to jump out. Auntie Beth is very nice really although she's not much of a talker. And I see what you mean about the verbs. That do seem a bit queer the way she talk, don't it!
It's rather miles from anywhere here. Not much point in going out as there's nowhere to get to as far as I can see. We went into Hadham (a town!) this morning, and I saw a nice fat young doctor, assistant to Dr. McTaggart who is some sort of top gyno—whatever the word is. Anyway, I go to his prenatal clinic on Thursday. It's something to look forward to, if nothing else. There is absolutely nothing to do here. Beth—she won't be called aunt—rushes about with buckets from the crack of dawn onward, but I can't even find out what she does, let alone help. She showed me around the farm today when we came back from Hadham, and it was a bit sad to see the milking parlor where the cows used to come in. She's still got cows, but not a milking herd, though she milks one by hand for the house. It's not as tatty as I expected, though. All rather neat and tidy, really. There are lovely geese with brown stripes down their

necks—Chinese, she says. Oh, and when we came back from the station last night, a cow was having a calf and we had to look at that before we even got into the house! Talk about being thrown in at the deep end! It was rather sweet, actually—not a bit messy except the calf was all wet.

We go to bed fearfully early. Although she's got a TV she never seems to watch it, but she reads a lot. Isn't *Cold Comfort Farm* a hoot! I feel a bit like Flora Poste, dumping myself on my relatives, though I can't decide if Beth is Aunt Ada Doom or Judith Starkadder.

If you have any bright ideas on how to pass the long hours, write and tell me. Write anyway—it'll be lovely to get a letter. Laurie had one in the post this morning, quick off the mark, though his didn't exactly cheer me up.

Lots of love, and to Nigel.

Kate.

She put the letter in an envelope, addressed it, and stuck on a stamp. Now she must write to Laurie. She had never written him a letter before, and she wished that her writing were not so round and untidy. It didn't even go along straight lines reliably, and compared with his elegant calligraphy it made her seem a mere schoolgirl. If only she had some *style*!

Dear Laurie,

Thank you for your marvelous letter. It's maddening, the way you do everything so well. Beautiful flowers, beautiful letter. No, I don't really mean maddening. It's just that I feel such a clumsy idiot in comparison.

I suppose the trouble is, I'm not much good at anything. I used to like art, but after I knew you I could see how bad my stuff was, and anyway it was more fun to watch you doing yours. And you always seemed to like me best when I was doing nothing, curled up in your lovely big leather armchair or lying on the floor listening to your old MJQ records.

Here I am chattering on when I ought to have said at the beginning thank you for giving me all that money. It's absolutely sweet of you, but honestly I don't think I will use it. Apart from anything else, Dr. Marsh says he wouldn't advise an abortion now—not that I asked him about it, because you know how I feel. I am *sorry* about it all, I really am. It seems as if it wasn't Meant, if you know what I mean. What with Barbara and then the baby, it just didn't seem possible to go on as we were before.

I don't quite know what I'm doing here. I suppose I'd still be at the Silver Snack Bar if I hadn't got the sack, but when that happened I just felt I had to get away from it all and give something else a chance to happen. It must sound awfully weak and inert to you, because you're such a great one for doing what you want—but I don't *know* what I want, you see. All I can do is wait and see what happens and then decide whether I like it. At the moment I don't like it here very much. It's very beautiful and I like the farm buildings because they're all in-and-outy with old pantiled roofs, a bit like the houses in Italy, but it's terribly boring. There's nobody to talk to except my aunt, and she doesn't say anything unless she has to. So that's why you're getting such a long letter. No, I don't just mean I'm writing to pass the time away.

It's the only way to talk to you as well. I'm writing this in bed and suddenly feel very sleepy.
Thank you again, darling.
Lots of love,
Your
Katie-cat.

6

When Kate came down the next morning, there were three men drinking tea in the kitchen. They stopped talking as Kate came in, and Beth said, "This is my niece, Kate, from London."

They nodded politely, and the youngest one of them smiled and asked, "Come for a country holiday, have you?"

Kate liked his lean face and the bright blue eyes under the mop of curly brown hair, but there was a trace of mockery in his question, and she suddenly resented being taken for a tourist "townie."

"Not exactly," she said coolly.

"Oh!" He was unrepentant. "Seems you've got a new farmhand then, Peter!"

The eldest of the men, thickset and gray-haired, gave him a reproving look, then introduced himself to Kate. "I'm Peter Thurlow. Live in the cottage up the lane. That cheeky young beggar is Alec Fairchild, and the other one's Tom, his father. Richest man in Suffolk, aren't you, Tom?"

"Wish I was," said Tom Fairchild, unruffled.

"You'll have Kate all in a muddle, you go on like that," said Beth. "Tom and Alec are millers," she explained. "Supply me with chicken pellets and all that. And they're our nearest neighbors. Their land border ours, over Cuckoo Wood way. Peter you'll see a bit of from time to time. He do all the arable work about here. When he's not drinking tea, that is."

Peter continued to sip his tea placidly, but Alec grinned and said, "Ooh, she's a hard boss is Mrs. Kennett! You want to watch it, Kate, or she'll have you out there with a muck fork!"

"I wouldn't mind," said Kate with bravado. "It's better than doing nothing."

A perplexed silence followed this statement, broken by Tom Fairchild, who regarded her with blue eyes like his son's and asked, "You've come here to live then, have you?"

This time Kate had made up her mind what to say. "Everyone's bound to know sooner or later, so I may as well say now. I'm going to have a baby. I'm not married and I was out of a job, so I dumped myself on Auntie Beth."

"Beth," corrected her aunt. "And you didn't dump yourself, I asked you."

There was a general stirring of cups and sipping of tea as the three men digested the information, not exchanging glances. Then Alec said, "Well, I think it takes courage to come out with it just like that, rather than leave it get around through gossip. Don't you, Dad?"

"Reckon that do," agreed his father, whose accent was much more strongly Suffolk than Alec's. "But if that'd been a girl of mine, I'd be after the young man in question, that I would!"

"Things are not that simple these days," said Beth reprovingly. "Times change, Tom. More tea?"

"Yes, please," said Peter.

The other two groaned, and Alec said, with a wink at Kate, "*Where* will Willow Farm barley be come harvest? Still in the sack, bor!"

"All right for you, Alec Fairchild," retorted Peter. "Takes a miller's son to ride about with his dad in the morning, instead of working like the rest of us!"

"Millers *and* farmers," corrected Alec with dignity. "And we're so well ahead with the planting we've got some time in hand. Not like some."

"Do you no good," said Peter, helping himself to sugar. "It'll be cold again before it's warm, and yours'll have its roots down no sooner than mine. You'll see."

With a sideways glance at Kate, Tom said, "So you've got a family again, Beth? That'll keep you at work for a while longer."

"Don't you start again, Tom Fairchild!" said Beth. "I'm not giving up farming until I have to, so you can put your money back in your pocket."

Tom shook his head regretfully and got to his feet.

"If I'm going to drop you in Hadham to pick up the Land-Rover, Alec," he said, "we'd best be moving."

"OK," said Alec. He stood up and Kate realized for the first time how tall he was. He smiled down at her. "Nice to have met you. I hope you'll like it here."

"I'm sure I will," said Kate, smiling back, "when I get used to it."

At the door he thought of something and turned back. "Look, if you want to go into town any time and Beth's busy, give us a ring. We often go that way, and one of us can most likely run you in."

"That *is* kind of you," said Kate gratefully. "I might take you up on that offer, because I'd hate to be bothering Beth all the time."

"Do that," said Alec.

When they had gone, Kate said, "It's nice to meet people. Wasn't it kind of him to offer me a lift?"

"They're all right, the Fairchilds," said Beth. "Tom's a good old boy. Young Alec's been a bit wild, but it seems as if he's settling down now. Taking some of the work off Tom's shoulders. They couldn't do nothing with him at school, mind. Being a farmer's son, he thought he had more interesting things to do. Never hardly went."

"That's like me," said Kate. "It seemed such a waste of time."

"There's always something you can learn," said Peter rather disapprovingly. He stood up and put his cup on the table.

"That may not be at school, though," observed Beth.

Peter put his cap on. "That may not," he agreed, and went out. Beth followed him, muttering something about Tom having no doubt left the sacks all higgledy-piggledy.

Alone in the kitchen, Kate washed the cups and emptied the teapot, then dried her hands slowly, staring out the window across the fields. Beth must often have stood looking out in the same way, she thought, and other women before her, back in the days of long skirts and sunbonnets, gazing at these same fields. It was easy to imagine an idyllic life here, with sunburned men sitting around the long table and white washing blowing under the pear tree. Ignoring the realities of winter and boredom, one could envisage a richly contented life involved with these fields that stretched to the sky, knowing each one as wheat or kale, barley or sugar beet, or grazing.

Kate shook her head. No use being sentimental about it. She had been born and brought up in London and back to London she would go in the fullness of time. And yet—she stared with a kind of yearning at the bare trees and the wind-torn gray sky—she wished that things were different.

The hospital corridor had dark-green tiles to shoulder level and was lit by fluorescent tubes running along the cream-painted arched ceiling. Kate thought of a poem she had read once that described a river as "a tunnel of green gloom." Just right, she thought, for this horrible hospital.

At every junction there were signposts pointing out *Path Lab*, *Orthopedic*, *Geriatric*, and other titles. Kate followed the ones that said *Prenatal* and found that they led her out of doors, round the side of a brick building with a pile of coke stacked against it, past a flight of stone steps running down to a basement door labeled *Morgue*, and at last through double doors into a separate building. A passage opened into a large waiting area where dozens of pregnant women sat on tubular steel chairs. Nearly all of them were knitting, and most of them were accompanied by at least one toddler. There was a thick, warm smell of diapers and stale milk.

"Got your card, dear?" asked the buxom nurse behind the desk.

Kate produced Dr. Marsh's letter, which the nurse opened and read.

"Fill in this form, dear, will you? You can sit down here at the desk."

Kate did as she was told. Name, address, age, marital status, maiden name, date of last monthly period, expected date of delivery, number of previous pregnancies. Husband's name, age, place of work. . . . "I don't think the rest of this applies to me," said Kate.

"Just sign it at the bottom, dear," said the nurse

with continued brightness. "I'll see if Mrs. Mack is free." She tapped at a pale-blue door, listened, and went in. After a few moments she came out, holding the door open for Kate. "Come along, Mrs. Carling."

"Miss."

"Everyone is Mrs. here. Give Mrs. Mack your form. Oh, got your specimen?"

"Yes." Kate rummaged for the rather large family-sized shampoo bottle that Beth had given her.

"Lovely!"

Nothing, Kate decided, would dampen that nurse's cheerfulness. She went in through the open door.

"Sit down," said the woman behind the desk, waving a pen but not looking up from the papers in front of her. Kate sat down. The room was very small and contained nothing but a filing cabinet, the desk, and the chairs either side of it. Mrs. Mack laid her pen neatly in a glass pen tray and leaned back in her chair. "Well," she said, taking off her glasses, "you're another of these modern young women." She smiled at her small witticism, but Kate, well-used to this kind of opening gambit from her school days, said nothing. She stared at Mrs. Mack with interest. Blue-rinsed gray hair, fat cheeks, small mouth, pearls. Turquoise polyester dress under the unbuttoned white coat. "Are you a doctor?" she asked.

"I am a social worker," said Mrs. Mack, as if announcing a far superior status. "Now. I see that you are not married." Again Kate said nothing. "Do you know who the baby's father is?" pursued Mrs. Mack.

"Of *course* I know!" said Kate furiously.

"You'd be surprised how many don't," said Mrs. Mack, picking up her pen. "What's his name?"

"What's that got to do with it?"

"It's got a lot to do with it!" retorted Mrs. Mack. "After all, he *is* the baby's father. Will he help you to maintain the child?"

"That's entirely between him and me," said Kate obstinately.

Mrs. Mack sighed. "We are only trying to help, you know. There's no need to take that sort of attitude."

Kate glared.

"What are your plans when you leave hospital?" continued Mrs. Mack. "Have you anywhere to live?"

"Yes, thanks."

"You do realize you will have to support yourself and the baby?"

"Yes."

"Are you qualified in any way? Or trained? Have you any work experience?"

"Plenty," said Kate.

"Of what kind?" Mrs. Mack looked more hopeful.

"I don't see that it matters," said Kate. "I'm not asking for any help. I'll manage."

"I admire your optimism," said Mrs. Mack coldly. She fished in her desk drawer. "This booklet tells you what benefits you are entitled to and explains about welfare foods. You'll find a form at the back to fill in—"

"Thanks," said Kate, taking the booklet. "Can I go now?"

Mrs. Mack gave her a long stare and then said heavily, "Yes, Miss Carling, you may."

The cheerful nurse looked up as Kate came out of the social worker's room. "Hello, dear. That didn't take long!"

"Quite long enough," said Kate grimly.

"Oh, dear. Well, I must admit, Mrs. Mack is a bit of a stick-in-the-mud," said the nurse. "You ought to have seen Mrs. Tovey; she's ever so nice. Or Miss Meredith. It just happened that it's Mrs. Mack's day on."

"I suppose I'd better get used to it," said Kate. "There must be lots of people who think unmarried mums are the lowest of the low."

"Lots of people want their heads examined," said the nurse firmly. "Now pop into a cubicle and get ready. Then I'll weigh and measure you."

"Get ready?"

"Tights and panties off or stockings rolled down."

"But I'm wearing jeans."

"Oh. So you are. You'll have to keep them on for today then. Just take them off as quickly as you can when you get into the consulting room. We mustn't keep the doctor waiting. Wear a skirt next time, though. It's much easier. Anyway, you won't fit into jeans much longer, will you?"

"No," said Kate, rather dismayed. "I suppose I won't." She had lived in jeans for years.

When she had been weighed and measured and the details had been written on her card, Kate went to join the other women in the waiting area. She found a chair beside a girl who was reading a book rather than knitting and who was not accompanied by toddlers. She wore a loose dress with long sleeves, and her fair hair was tied back in a bun except for bangs as thick as Kate's own. Altogether she looked a less alarming neighbor than the rabble of old hands congregated on the front seats, shouting amiably to each other above the din of their bawling, blanket-waving, sweet-eating offspring.

"I'm having me teeth out next week," one woman yelled conversationally to her friend. "All the top ones. He says they won't last much longer, and I may as well get it done while it's free."

"That's what I did last time," agreed the friend. "Save a lot, don't it?"

Kate's neighbor glanced up from her book and caught Kate's own glance with a gleam of horrified amusement. She looked clever, Kate thought, observing the clear gray eyes under the blond bangs. The book on her lap was called *Italian in Six Weeks.*

"That's energetic," said Kate. "Learning Italian?"

"Not really. It's just that being pregnant made me feel such a *cabbage*. Do you speak Italian?"

"Oh, no," said Kate. "Well, just a few words. I've been to Italy once or twice. I ought to have learned more, really."

"Lucky thing! I wondered for a moment if you *were* Italian. You almost might be, with that dark hair. Whereabouts have you been?"

"To a village not far from Lucca, in the Tuscan hills."

"Oh, how marvelous. It's a sort of dream of mine, going to Italy. Is this your first baby?"

"Yes," said Kate.

"Mine, too. We've always wanted children, but we've been married six years without producing any, and I got used to the idea that we never would. When I found I was pregnant, I was delighted, of course, and yet I felt sort of—caught out. Do you know what I mean?"

"Oh, yes," said Kate.

"But Michael's absolutely thrilled," the girl went on. "It'll be so marvelous for him to be a father."

"Why didn't you go to Italy before?" asked Kate, changing the subject. "If you hadn't any children and weren't tied—"

"Michael works for an agricultural supplies firm," explained the girl. "In the summer he has to go to all the county shows, demonstrating equipment, and I was teaching, so we couldn't go any other time. He's mad about skiing, though, so we always went abroad at Christmas."

"Lovely," said Kate. She found herself envious. It must be wonderful to have an adoring, successful, winter-sporting husband who was thrilled about the baby.

"What does your husband do?" asked the girl suddenly.

Caught off guard, Kate said impulsively, "He's a graphic designer."

"What a marvelous thing to be! Does he turn out tons of beautiful drawings for record albums and that sort of thing?"

Kate laughed. "That sort of thing, yes." It had been sharply revealed to her just what it meant to be married. Basking in fictitious complacency, she felt for a moment the pleasure of being an insider, a club member. And why not? There was no need to bare one's soul to every casual acquaintance, was there?

Kate could hear Laurie's rather high-pitched yelp of laughter at the suggestion. "No need?" he would say. "Good heavens, dear, soul baring is absolutely suicidal!"

"What's his name?"

"M'm?" Kate had lost track of her questioner's train of thought.

"Your husband. What's his name?"

"Oh, Laurie." Kate had very nearly said Laurie

Coppersmith, but realized in the nick of time that she was called Mrs. Carling in this hospital. That would make Laurie into Mr. Carling. He would be *furious*!

"What's your other name? Mine's Cooney, by the way. Tessa Cooney."

"Carling. Kate Carling." Kate began to wish she had accepted Laurie's offer of his surname. The hospital, with its muffling tea cozy of convention, had thrown her into a fiction that was already difficult to sustain. Supposing Laurie came to see her when the baby was born? He would no doubt demand to see his wife, Mrs. Coppersmith. Kate sighed to herself. Perhaps soul baring was easier in the long run.

"Mrs. Cooney!" called an Indian nurse, consulting a list of names on a clipboard.

"Oh, good." Tessa Cooney slipped her Italian book into her bag and stood up. "See you again, no doubt." She smiled and added, "You and Laurie must come over and have a drink with us some time."

Kate was saved from having to reply to this embarrassing invitation by the Indian nurse, who said rather sharply, "Come along, Mrs. Cooney, dear! Doctor's waiting!" Doctors, Kate began to realize, must never, never be kept waiting.

In the consulting room, Kate removed the offending jeans at top speed. She scrambled onto the couch, slipped off her pants, and lay down on the disposable paper sheet, covering herself with a pink blanket that the Indian nurse handed to her. She lay there for quite a long time, and then a tall, gray-haired doctor came in.

"How are you feeling?"

"All right," said Kate. The doctor was scrutinizing the notes on his clipboard.

"Willow Farm?" He spoke with a marked Scottish accent. "You're staying with Mrs. Kennett?"

"Yes."

"Are you a relative of some sort?"

"I'm her niece."

The doctor stared at her through his steel-rimmed glasses, bushy eyebrows knitted. "Whose daughter are you then?"

"My father's name is Rowley."

"Rowley Carling's girl! Well, I'm blessed. I haven't seen him for many a long year. Where's he living now?"

"In Australia. He and Mum split up when I was quite small."

"Dear, dear, dear. You find so much of that nowadays. He married an actress, didn't he?"

"Yes, Nancy Flynn. She still uses her maiden name professionally. You might have seen her on television."

"Oh. So she's a film star, is she?"

Kate laughed. "I wish she were! No, she never really hit the big time. She gets pretty steady work, though, and she teaches a bit."

"In a school?"

"No, she has a Saturday morning group of children for LAMDA exams, and she does evening classes in voice production and verse speaking, and a mime session at Floral Street."

"Good gracious. So she's too busy to look after you?"

"No, it's not that." Kate was finding it difficult to talk lying flat on her back so she propped herself on one elbow. The doctor's name, she saw from the tag on his white coat, was McTaggart. The big white chief himself. "There just didn't seem to be anything to stay in London for."

Dr. McTaggart glanced at his watch, and Kate, remembering all the other women standing outside, lay down again.

"So you're a lady of leisure?" said Dr. McTaggart, turning back the pink blanket.

Kate was stung by the description and retorted, "I was working until last week, and I've been here only four days!"

"Yes. Just relax." He examined Kate's abdomen, feeling the growing thickness with warm, firm fingers. "Right." He replaced the blanket. "Are you taking any iron?"

"No."

"We'll give you some tablets before you go." He stared at Kate with pursed lips. "Why did you choose Willow Farm to come to?"

There was something disapproving about his question. Feeling rather aggrieved, Kate said, "There wasn't any choice, really. And Beth seemed quite willing to have me. Mum said she thought she was lonely."

"Lonely!" Dr. McTaggart gave a bark of laughter. "No, no. Beth Kennett is not a seeker of human company. And I must say, as I get older I am inclined to agree with her. Did you know your aunt had a heart attack three years ago?"

"No, I didn't."

"Aye. She had a bad time of it. I told her she should give up the farm, but she wouldn't. She sold the milking herd, though." He shot Kate an accusing glance. "I dare say she told you they went when Jack died?"

"No, I don't think so. I don't remember that she mentioned it."

"M'm." Dr. McTaggart pulled at his lip, looking troubled. "I don't want her doing too much."

Kate lost her temper. She sat up and said, "You don't have to worry. I'm not going to be a drag on *anyone*. I don't *want* to be a lady of leisure, and I'd get a job tomorrow, but the godforsaken place is miles from anywhere, and I can't drive. And anyway, if people want to be heroes, it's not my fault. I'm not even sure if I *like* Willow Farm, and if I don't, then I'll shove off and live somewhere else."

He grinned at her scarlet face and the mop of tousled hair and said, "All right, my dear, I'm sorry. I dare say you and your aunt will work things out between you. She's not a woman to beat about the bush anymore than you are, it seems!"

Kate's rage began to subside. "I think she'd say if I were getting on her nerves," she said.

"I'm sure she would. Now your problem is going to be boredom, isn't it, out there at the farm? See if you can get her to let you help a bit. She could do with a hand, God knows, and a healthy young woman like you can get through a fair bit of work with no harm whatever. Do you get much sickness?"

"Just in the mornings."

"Yes. In another week or two you should find that easing off a bit. It doesn't usually persist through the middle months of pregnancy, and there's no point in doling out drugs for a wee bit of nausea. Now we won't need to see you for another four weeks. It'll be three weeks after that, then two, then we'll see you each week until the baby's born." He strode across the room and paused with his hand on the door handle. "Plenty of fresh air and exercise. And give my regards to your aunt." Then he was gone.

Kate pulled on her pants rather crossly. Plenty of fresh air and exercise, indeed! Country life with a vengeance. She was lucky to have got away without being dipped and sheared.

The Indian nurse bustled in. "Quick as you can, dear, so the next lady can come in. Mustn't keep Doctor waiting."

7

In the days following the hospital visit, Kate tried hard to find ways to occupy the long hours. Her offers of help were received evasively by Beth, and Kate sensed that she would do no good by trying to force assistance upon her. She trailed about after her aunt, watching what she did and trying to grasp the routine of her work, but Beth did not talk to her much. She went about her tasks in an absorbed, contented ritual that for years had needed no words except the occasional "Git over!" and Kate understood that talking would distract her from what she was doing.

Thrown back on her own resources, she walked down the muddy lane to the village shop two miles away and bought some knitting wool and a book of patterns called *Everything for Baby.* The woman in the shop asked, "Are you a beginner, dear?"

"Oh, yes," Kate answered. "At babies *and* knitting."

The woman had regarded her gravely and said she would be all right with that book then. That weren't meant for experts.

But Kate found knitting an irritating occupation. The slightest absentmindedness resulted in a chaotic muddle and besides it involved a lot of counting, and Kate seldom reached a total without having lost track of the number of stitches. Was it seventy-six or eighty-six? She would push the whole lemon-yellow bundle back into its bag, jump up restlessly, and go to the window to look out. She never tired of staring at the sweeping lines of the fields and the expanse of sky. After the confined aspects of London, there was a magnetic fascination about such emptiness. Sometimes she found it forbidding and was glad to turn away to the warmth of the enclosed room, but the knowledge that it was out there, vast and open and windswept, intrigued her continually, and before long she would go to the window to look out again.

For the sake of something to do she swept and dusted and polished, taking pleasure in seeing the old house bright and clean. "Funny, that," observed Beth. "I was just the same each time I was having a baby. Always had things clean as a new pin. I suppose that's natural, like a cat wash herself all over before she have kittens. Not so much risk of infection when things are clean." This was a long speech for Beth, and Kate was absurdly pleased. Conversation was a rare pleasure nowadays, and she had learned to value it.

The days went by very slowly, with little to distinguish one from the next except the arrival of letters.

Kate's mother wrote in a cheerful, breathless sort of way, jotting down fragments of gossip and funny anecdotes interspersed with news of Nigel and their plans for married life. One letter announced that the house in Finchley was up for sale. "Don't worry, darling," Nancy wrote, "all your things will be lovingly stored at Nigel's until you want them, and there's a dear little spare bedroom if you decide to come and live with us. Did you ever see Nigel's house? I don't think you did. It's at Highgate, as you know, a nice, quiet road not too far from the Park." It sounded very unattractive, Kate thought.

There were letters from school friends, too, Sandie and Lorna and Chris, who had rung up and been told that Kate was staying with her aunt. They wanted to know when she was coming back and whether she was enjoying her "away from it all" spree. And Chris, with an inspired guess, wrote, "It sounds as if you've gone into retreat to have a baby or something. Do tell me if you are. I'd be fascinated." Kate wrote back and told her. She told Sandie and Lorna, too, and had such concerned, affectionate letters in return that she felt ashamed of not confiding in them earlier, before she had come away.

Laurie's letters were graceful and world-weary.

I find myself increasingly sought after, which is gratifying but not enjoyable. For I seek the freedom to set my own standards rather than continue to turn out a profitable but dull Coppersmith self-parody. If these idiot publishers really want value for money they should pay me to develop the other good things which lie unborn within me. Speaking of which, how is my Josephine faring? For I am sure it will be a girl, an elfin child who will grow to be a fascinating woman. . . .

Kate sighed. It was more and more difficult to answer Laurie's letters. She had absolutely nothing to tell him except the details of how she felt and what she was doing, and he would find these ludicrously trivial.

I cleaned out the cow shed after Beth had finished milking today. She told me to go "behind the broom and in front of the hose," and I found out what she meant when I did it. If you sweep ahead of you, you don't tread in your own dirt, and if you hose behind you, you wash off your own muddy boot marks!

But she had torn that letter up. Laurie would shout with contemptuous laughter, and how could a creative person like him be expected to share her absurd pleasure in learning such a mundane skill? Perhaps, too, it was a pleasure she didn't really *want* to share.

There was a funny letter from Annie at the Silver Snack Bar, written in a sprawling childish hand on a bit of lined paper torn from an exercise book.

Dear Kate here I must tell you you remember Mrs. Heath well she got the sack they say she had her hand in the till all that time what a laugh bet you wish youd known when you were there hows the baby coming on pop in and see us when you had it cheers Annie.

Kate showed that one to Beth, who grinned, said, "She's not much on full stops, is she?" and went out to chop some wood for the Aga.

It really was a bit like Cold Comfort Farm sometimes, Kate thought. There was a kind of leathery simplicity about Willow Farm that made Laurie's creative struggles seem effete. There was, too, an acceptance of reality that made any complaint unthinkable. Beth had never once referred to the heart attack that Dr. McTaggart had told Kate about, and although she sometimes got up rather stiffly from her chair after a meal, she said no more than, "A bit rheumaticky. Be nice when spring come."

But spring showed no sign of coming. An east wind whipped across the fields, finding every crack in the old buildings and penetrating the thick-walled house through window frames and under doors. "Best get the cold over now than have it spoil the blossom in May," Beth said sturdily. But Kate felt depressed. Sluggish with inactivity, she was constantly cold and noticed with gloomy envy that Beth seemed to glow with warmth when she came in from working outside. In self-defense, Kate put on boots, parka, and woolly hat and went out with her aunt every time she left the house. It was not easy to find anything that wanted doing. Without appearing to hurry, Beth was constantly on her way to the next job, leaving Kate standing awkwardly in cow shed or feed store, never in the right place at the right time and never knowing which buckets to fill with what. She began to realize how totally ignorant she was of the commonplace ways and means of farm work. Nothing was without a tiny element of common sense that made it simpler and yet gave it an element of right-and-wrong that Kate had never suspected.

One day Beth handed Kate the fat clasp knife that she carried in her pocket saying, "Cut the strings on the bale for me." Kate was delighted to be given something to do and enjoyed the way the released hay sprang from its bindings. "Hang the strings on that nail," her aunt instructed, indicating a thick hank of orange twine against the wall.

Kate, tugging ineffectually, found that the knots in the string were stuck under the bale and would not pull through the weight of tight-packed hay. "Aren't they awkward!" she said.

"They are if you don't cut them right," agreed Beth. "You find the knots first before you cut. Then you've only got to pull the loose ends out, and it come easy."

It was the same with gates. Each one had its own particular technique, needing to be lifted a bit or wedged with a brick kicked under it or fastened with a wooden peg, which had to be cut to shape again if you broke it. And one evening Beth came near to being irritable when she had to put her buckets down and take both hands to untie a door that Kate had fastened with string.

"Is there a peg or something I should have used?" asked Kate nervously.

"No, that do with string," Beth said, "but for goodness' sake tie a knot that pull out easy." And she showed Kate how to tie a knot like half a bow, so that a tug at the loose end released it.

"Sorry," said Kate.

"That's all right," said her aunt. "You'll learn."

Almost imperceptibly Kate did learn. She began to know the sequence of the morning routine, feeding poultry, milking the house cow, then putting her calf in to suckle, feeding the ewes in the covered yard, then the bullocks and the suckler cows and calves. Mangers had to be filled with hay or barley straw, yards littered, water tanks checked, and chicken drinkers cleaned and refilled. The milk for the house was filtered and poured into a big jug to put in the fridge, any remaining from the previous day going out to the two little pigs that lived in a warm shed near the feed store. This shed was mucked out every few days, an easy job as the pigs never made a mess of the clean straw where they slept.

Compared with the tedious, repetitive jobs Kate had done in London, she found farm work varied and enjoyable. Peter Thurlow looked in at the yard each morning before he started work with the tractor and made sure there was no heavy lifting or carrying to be done. "You two are bad as each other," he would grumble. "Got no idea how to look after yourselves, neither of you." Kate glowed with pleasure at being included with Beth in this way, but privately she thought the work fairly easy and could not see why Dr. McTaggert had been so anxious about Beth's welfare.

One day Beth seemed to read Kate's thoughts and said, "I reckon you think there's not much to stock keeping. Couple of two hours morning and evening, and you're done. You'll see a difference in a week or two, though. We start lambing on the fifteenth, and then there're a good many cows to calve and the poultry all start breeding in the spring. This is the lull before the storm, you might say."

Kate remembered the calving she had seen on the night she arrived, a calm affair that demanded no particular attention, and wondered why Beth thought it worth mentioning. But she welcomed the thought of increased activity, for despite her efforts to help, a lot of time remained unfilled, and she had an odd sense of shame in being indoors. Beth's attitude to the house was quite different from her involvement with the farm. To be inside was to be not working, even though there were domestic jobs to be done. The house was basically a warm refuge in which to kick off boots, to eat and sleep, to write letters at the fireside, do the accounts, and catch up with the news in the *East Anglian Daily Times*.

Quite often Kate felt happy and involved, but there were days when she was deeply depressed. Her waistline was perceptibly thicker now and bending down made her feel breathless. Her jeans would not do up, and she had secured them with a large safety pin, which sometimes came undone. Since the weather was so cold, she wore long, baggy sweaters and had not yet thought about the problem of what to wear when the days turned warmer. The spring seemed a long way off, and on bad days she felt imprisoned in tedium and loneliness.

One such day came in early March, when Kate had been at the farm just over three weeks. She had awakened to find the fields white with snow, the leaden sky shredding into blizzard. Winter was back again. Beth's face was redder than usual as she came in with her bucket of milk. "That's coming quite thick," she observed, taking off her head scarf and shaking it into the sink.

"Yes," said Kate. She ached all over with a heavy tiredness that made her want to weep. She thought nostalgically of London where it was never so cold as it was here. In London when the pavements were wet they shone with reflected lights from shopwindows and there were places to escape into. Big stores, carpeted and smelling of cosmetics and bedspreads. Coffeehouses. Pubs. Buses. But she hated it, too. Buses had queues waiting for them, and everything cost a lot of money. Everything was cold and unhappy. How crazy it was to bring a child into such a dismal world. What a dreadful mistake.

Beth fished a milk filter out of the packet. She glanced at Kate and said, "Do you feel all right?"

"Yes," said Kate. She had learned something of Beth's resilience but felt that she could never be tough enough to cope with life at Willow Farm. She didn't hate it—in a way she almost loved it—but she didn't belong. Beth had run the place without help for years. She didn't need Kate. She didn't seem to need anybody. There was no point in staying here, struggling to be part of something that was quite indifferent to her very existence. It would be better to go back to London and hope that her mother was not too involved with Nigel to have time for her. Or perhaps she could put aside her worries about living with Laurie. Surely he would get used to the baby in time?

A car came into the yard, headlights beaming through the driving snow.

"That'll be Mr. Clark with the post," said Beth. "I don't suppose Mrs. Willisham can make it on her bike."

"I'll go and see," said Kate in a sudden desperate yearning for a letter. She went into the yard, pulling her parka hood up against the snow, as Mr. Clark was turning the car around.

"Hello, dear," he said cheerfully. "Nasty morning. Here we are." He handed Kate a handful of letters and the morning paper through the car window. "And a parcel," he said. "That's addressed to you. Hope it's something nice. Bye-bye!" He drove off with a wave and a rather wild slewing of the back wheels. Kate went back to the kitchen.

"I reckon you're homesick," said Beth. Kate stared at the letters in her hand, the uppermost of which was in her mother's writing. It was no good. She *was* going to cry. A tear trickled down her cheek and onto the letter. She rubbed it off angrily with her sleeve.

"You don't have to stay, my dear," said Beth in her deliberate fashion. "Not if that's making you unhappy. I'd miss you, mind."

"You wouldn't," blurted Kate. "You don't need me. Nobody does." She put her hands over her face and gave up all attempt to restrain her tears. Beth came over to where she stood and put her arms around her, stroking Kate's unruly hair.

"Come on, my lovely," she said, "I know how you feel. You get bad days when you're pregnant. You sit down here, and I'll put the kettle on. You haven't had a cup of tea this morning yet, have you?"

With the kettle spitting on the Aga, Beth came and sat down beside Kate. "You see," she said, "I'd be a silly woman to start depending on a young thing who's only staying a month or two, wouldn't I? Just think what a muddle I'd be in when you left."

"Yes," admitted Kate, gulping. "I know that. And I want to stay here really. It's just– There's nothing to do."

Beth considered this. "I can see what you mean," she said. "But you've learned a lot, haven't you? I was thinking the other day, you're quite handy round the place now." She thought a bit longer, then said, "How would you like to run the poultry? Take it over altogether. Feed them and collect the eggs and see to the egg sales. And when they start going broody, you can set the hens and look after the incubator and rear the chicks."

"Oh! Do you think I could?"

"Not without a bit of telling, but you'd learn. Starting now while there's not much going on, you'd get used to it easily."

"I'd love to try," said Kate, "if you really wouldn't mind."

"That would be a help to me," said Beth. "Lambing start quite soon now, and I'd be glad to get a job off my hands."

"What about when I have the baby, though? I'll be away in hospital, and then I suppose I'll go back to London."

Beth gave one of her rare smiles. "I expect I'll manage," she said. She retrieved her head scarf from the back of the chair where she had left it and went out, followed by the old dog, Glyn.

Kate sorted the letters. There were three for Beth, and she put them on the dresser where she would find them. The other two were addressed to herself, one from her mother as she already knew, and one from Laurie. And there was the parcel. She opened her mother's letter first.

Dear Katie,
Your last letter made Nigel and me feel worried about you. It all sounded so depressing and boring—mind you, pregnancy *does* give you the most ghastly days of gloom, I remember. Perhaps it's the hormones or something. If you can stick it out for a week or two, we'll have things a bit more organized but just now it's pretty chaotic. We've got a buyer for the Finchley house, and his wife is driving me mad popping in and out with a tape measure all the time and asking silly questions about drains. We want to sell some of the furniture so that Nigel's house won't burst at the seams (he's selling some of his, too), but I keep having miseries about parting with things and there have been tetchy little quarrels about whose sideboard is nicest. Nigel is so sweet, though, I always win. I'm doing a commercial for *polish* next week—me, of all people, can you imagine! But lots of lovely money. Sorry this all seems to be about me and I meant to write about you. I know you've got heaps of determination at heart, so hang on for a little while, darling, then we'll come and rescue you.
All my love,
M.
PS. Nigel has just come in and says why don't we drive down and see you this weekend? Sounds a lovely idea. Sunday would be best because of my LAMDA kids, so expect us about midday and we'll take you out to lunch. Beth too. Till then,
M.

Kate felt that she had had a narrow escape. It would have been awful if she had actually written to her mother asking if she could come home, because the answer would clearly have been No. Laurie's letter was shorter.

My dear,
Barbara died last night.
Unexpectedly, I feel very upset. After all, she was my wife. In a way, I am glad at the moment that I am living alone. The impact of the guilt and remorse that I feel would have put an intolerable strain on our relationship. I know you will understand what I mean.
Time heals, they say. For both of us, I hope so.
With all tender feelings,
Laurie.

Kate put the two letters together tidily. So that was that. There was no decision to be made, after all. Quite plainly, she would stay in Suffolk until the baby was born. Her mother's talk of "a week or two" more realistically meant "a month or two" if not more. She stood up, opened the fire door of the Aga, and poked both letters in, where they burned away at once. She dumped some coke on top of their glowing ghosts and slammed the door shut. Then she turned to the parcel.

It contained a box of watercolor paints, some brushes, a sketch pad, a Rapidograph, some ink, and a lot of felt-tip pens. A note with it said, "Dear Kate. We thought it might be a bit boring waiting for the Event, so we got you these. Mr. Hepworth advised us on what to get and sends his best wishes. Lots of love, Sandie, Lorna, and Chris."

Kate was deeply touched. How *nice* of them! She fingered the enticing blank paper and was tempted to sit down at once and try out all the deliciously untouched new colors. But at that moment Beth came in carrying two galvanized poultry drinkers, which were frozen completely solid.

"Here you are," she said. "You can make a start on your poultry. Put these under the tap and get them thawed out."

Suddenly Kate was feeling much better.

That afternoon she spread out her new art materials on the kitchen table. She filled the Rapidograph with its special ink and drew a wavering, wiry line with it. Then she drew a flower and colored it pink and orange and mauve with the new, free-running felt-tip pens. She gave a little sigh of pleasure, which was followed at once by a feeling of duty toward all these beautiful tools. She must find something worthwhile to do with them. Merely to scribble patterns did not use their potential. But what should she draw?

Kate thought back to Mr. Hepworth's art lessons and the frequent complaints from his pupils. "Sir, I don't know how to do it." "Of *course* you don't," he would retort. "None of us do. That's the whole fascination of the thing, puzzling out a way to put down what you see. You're not a camera. Good grief, no human being will ever be a mechanical device that reels off snapshots, *click–click*–God forbid!" Everyone giggled and the boys did obscene drawings, which they turned over quickly at Mr. Hepworth's approach. He didn't mind, though. "If your head is stuffed with genitalia, lad, draw it by all means," he said. "Art is a personal statement. That's *your* personal statement." So after a bit more giggling, most people got on with the subject he had suggested.

Kate stared out the window. A personal statement. The paved yard had low buildings along two sides, with stable doors and pantiled roofs patterned in black and white scallops now because of the light covering of snow. The last building was the cow shed, whose roof came to a triangular pitch topped by a carved wooden spike. Behind it was a huge willow tree and the pond where the ducks would be swimming if it wasn't frozen over, and beyond the hedge and five-barred gate was a field and then more fields, running up the sloping hillside until they met the gray sky.

Kate had never been quite sure how perspective was supposed to work. "Oh, that's just a mechanical trick," Laurie had said dismissively. "Any twit can pick that up in ten minutes flat."

And Mr. Hepworth had beaten his fist on his forehead despairingly. "Why *will* people clutter their minds with these technical obsessions? They put up screens of conventional expectations, and it stops them seeing. Look how Giotto saw, and the Douanier Rousseau, and the unknown men who painted in caves! Stare curiously at your surroundings, Kate, as if you were a kitten with newly opened eyes, staring at the inside of a cardboard box. Brown. Rough. Strange. But *see* it—*see* it!"

Thinking of the kitten, Kate stared. The nice thing about the view from the window, she thought, was the way the fields sloped down to hold the farm in a hollow. The buildings were busy with small patterns made sharp by the white areas of snow: brick on brick, stone beside stone. And the mad little spike on the cow-shed roof came in the middle of the curving lines of hedges, almost as if they were joined to it. The willow tree would fit better into the design if it was moved to the right a bit, so that it's trunk came clear of the cow shed.

Kate began to draw.

8

For the two days following the birth of the first lamb, Kate suspected that Beth never went to bed. Peter Thurlow came up to the house, and, despite Kate's offer of help, it was his assistance that Beth accepted. Kate did not mind. Peter was experienced and she was not, and besides she felt very tired in the evenings and was glad to cuddle into her warm bed. She listened to the deep mutter of the ewes and the lambs' high-pitched bleating and could not imagine what was involved in looking after them. When she switched off her bedside lamp, the light in the covered yard made an unaccustomed pale stripe across her ceiling, and when she woke once at dead of night it was still there.

She went down to the kitchen the next morning to find Beth putting a nipple on a bottle of milk. "*There* you are!" she was greeted. "Just the person. You'll want to get your hand in with a feeding bottle." A tiny lamb lay in front of the Aga, watched over by old

Glyn, who licked it protectively from time to time. "Oh, dear," said Kate. "Has it's mother died?"

"No, it's one of triplets," said Beth. "I always take one away if it's triplets. A ewe has only two teats, you see."

Bottle in hand, Kate knelt beside the lamb, which bleated loudly when she touched it.

"Sit in the armchair with it," advised Beth. "Easier that way. And put a towel under it, or it'll pee all over you."

The lamb sucked vigorously for a little while, then lost interest. "You were right about the towel," said Kate. She replaced the lamb on the hearthrug and inspected the bottle. "It's had about a quarter of a pint."

"Good," said Beth, stirring two mugs of tea. "Stand the bottle in some hot water. It'll want some more later. I'll take this out to Peter."

It seemed colder than ever when Kate went out to feed her poultry. The hens stood in the shelter of their open-sided barn with their feathers fluffed up disconsolately, but when Kate approached with her buckets of feed they came running, pecking ravenously at the pellets and grain that rattled on the frozen ground. The ducks seemed less affected by the cold, but they, too, were hungry. The mallards took to their wings as the quickest way to reach the food, and their flat feet skidded absurdly on landing. The Aylesburys and Khaki Campbells simply pushed in wherever they could, shoveling up the grain at top speed. Beth contended that free-range poultry were best fed on the ground. "That encourage them to forage," she explained. "And besides, that stop anyone hogging the lot." Looking at the gobbling ducks, Kate could see her point. She liked the ducks, though. They would glance up sometimes, head on one side, as if they were really looking at her, whereas the other birds were always preoccupied with their own affairs. The geese were as noisy and aggressive as a street gang, and the guinea fowls tiptoed about like walking lampshades, their spotted feathers hanging in a mad fringe over their skinny legs. And there was just one turkey, a hesitant, rather poetic-looking creature with purply-brown feathers scalloped with white. Her mincing walk and tiny head gave her the look of an Edwardian lady who has found herself among ruffians but is trying nevertheless to preserve decent standards of behavior.

Kate took the frozen drinkers indoors and dumped them in the sink. She gave the lamb a little more milk and was pleased to find that it sucked much more energetically, shaking its long tail with delight. She put it back by the fire, but when she went over to the sink to fill the poultry drinkers, the lamb tottered after her, bleating. Glyn got stiffly to his feet and nosed the lamb back to the hearthrug, then flopped down with one heavy paw across it. Kate smiled. He was obviously used to this job. She filled the drinkers with warm water and took them outside.

The lambing yard was strident with bleating. There was a row of pens along one wall made of wooden hurdles, and some of the sheep were in them. Most were loose in the yard, some lying contentedly with their lambs beside them, others feeding from the trough and hayrack that ran along another wall. The feeding ones called incessantly to their lambs, turning their heads anxiously while still keeping up their rapid munching. Seeing Beth bending over a ewe in one of the pens, Kate called, "Hello! How's it going?"

"Pretty well," said Beth. "Only two more to lamb from this bunch. The others will be later."

"How do you know?" asked Kate.

Her aunt straightened up. "The ram has a bag of colored dye strapped under him so when he mounts a ewe he marks her with that color. A ewe come in season every three weeks, so after three weeks we change the color. So any ewes he missed the first time or that didn't hold service get marked with the new color, and you know they'll lamb later."

"Isn't that clever!" said Kate, impressed by this unexpectedly long lecture. Looking around, she added, "Is there anything I can do? What about the other animals?"

"Peter's doing them," said Beth, bending over the ewe again. "This old girl seem in a bit of a muddle. Could you get me a bucket of warm water, please, Kate?"

"Yes, of course."

When Kate came back with the bucket, Beth scrubbed her hands and arms and covered them with a clear jelly poured from a plastic bottle. Then, very carefully, she felt inside the straining ewe. "My goodness," she said, eyes shut with concentration, "she's got them in a right old knot. Triplets again, I think. . . ." Kate watched in fascinated suspense as Beth pushed and sorted, her red face redder than ever with effort. "*That's* better," she said. The ewe strained again, and Beth brought her hand out slowly, holding a lamb by its front feet, helping the ewe to push it out. It came quickly once the head was through and lay wet and inert on the straw.

"Is it alive?" asked Kate fearfully.

"Don't know," said Beth, busy inside the ewe again. "Wash your hands thoroughly in that bucket, then clear its mouth of mucus, and give it a rub."

Kate did as she was told. To her joy, the little tongue moved and the lamb uttered a bubbling bleat. Beth delivered the next lamb, and the third was born easily without assistance. The ewe scrambled to her feet and began to lick the lambs, muttering to them in the peculiar deep voice that Kate had never heard them use at any other time.

"Should I take one lamb indoors?" she asked.

"Later on. All three want a good feed from the ewe first."

"Why?"

"They need the colostrum. That make the newborn thing able to digest protein, you see, and give it antibodies to protect it from germs. And it's a concentrated foodstuff."

"Isn't that marvelous! Is it the same for humans?"

"Of course it is. Didn't they teach you *anything* at school?"

"Not really," said Kate. Then she added with honesty, "They did try, though."

Beth splashed each lamb's severed cord with iodine, then replaced her pots and bottles in a clean bucket. She loaded a hypodermic syringe with whitish fluid, parted the ewe's fleece carefully, and injected her.

"What's that for?" asked Kate.

"Antibiotics in case of infection because I had to help her," explained Beth. "Now let's get things cleaned up. Take the syringe for me. That'll need boiling." She picked up her bucket and held the hurdle aside for Kate to go out in front of her. She looked very tired, Kate thought, and no wonder.

"Do you ever get a holiday?" she asked.

"Jack and I used to," said Beth. "We'd go up to Scotland after harvest. He liked fishing. We went on a cruise once, but I didn't much care for that. Too many people."

"But you never get a break now?"

"Don't really want to. Whatever would I do with myself?"

"I just thought you must get awfully tired."

"Sometimes," Beth admitted. "But a good night's sleep soon put me right again."

Kate laughed. But she was not so sure.

Nancy Carling came into the kitchen huddled waif-like in the cobweb-fine shawl that Kate had last seen her wearing in Finchley. Curls of pale red hair escaped beautifully from their careless pinning, enhancing the effect of storm-driven frailty. "I thought we'd *never* get here," she said.

"Bit of trouble map reading," explained Nigel.

"Hello, Mum," said Kate.

"Darling." Her mother enfolded her warmly. "How are you?"

"I'm fine," said Kate.

"Glass of sherry?" offered Beth, bottle in hand. "Warm you up."

"Good idea," said Nigel.

Nancy sank into an armchair and accepted a glass. "Cheers." She sipped, gazed round the room, and smiled. "What a lovely old place this is. You are *lucky*, Beth."

"Yes?" said Beth.

"I mean," Nancy persisted, "life must be so satisfying. Doing your own thing."

"I reckon everybody do that," said Beth. "No one else's fault if they don't, is it?"

Nigel said, "Is there anywhere open for lunch? It's nearly half past two."

"We ought to have got up earlier," lamented Nancy. "Once you leave civilization you can never find anywhere open."

Kate looked at Beth and grinned. There were two ducks roasting in the oven. Beth had said, "If they get here on time, we can have them cold, but I don't reckon they will." Distentangling which *they* was which, Kate had laughed and agreed.

"Shall I set the table?" she asked.

"Yes, please," said Beth. "And grate some nutmeg on that trifle while I make the gravy."

Nancy sighed. "These country dwellers make you sick, don't they?" she said. "All this self-sufficiency and independence. We did at least bring some wine—Nigel, dear, would you get it out of the car?—and it *isn't* homemade."

"Good," said Beth.

Lunch lingered pleasantly into the afternoon, and Nigel, who had helped himself rather liberally to the wine, fell asleep with his feet stretched out blissfully by the Aga.

"You can't take him anywhere," said Nancy.

"That's what most men do Sunday afternoons," said Beth, getting to her feet. Kate got up, too.

"What are you going to do now?" inquired Nancy. "Something fascinatingly agricultural?"

"Animals' time," said Kate. "My chickens will go to sleep when it gets dark, so I must feed them while it's still daylight. Oh, and you must come and see the lambs, Mum."

"Where are they?" asked Nancy cautiously.

"In a little shed just by the back door. They used to be in here, but they're much stronger now."

Nancy consented to watch Kate feed the lambs and agreed that they were sweet. She gazed at the two eagerly sucking little animals and gave a shiver, hugging herself more closely in her shawl. "Don't they take a long time!" she said.

"They're much quicker than they were," said Kate. "Do you want to come and see the poultry? I'm sure Beth can lend you some Wellies."

"No, thank you, dear," said Nancy firmly. She looked at her daughter with curiosity. "Things must have changed," she said. "Just a few days ago you sounded so depressed that Nigel and I were really worried. And I could understand why. I mean, all this icy cold and muck and being miles from anywhere. And Beth's so—well—blunt. Admittedly it was a delicious lunch, but I still think the place is a bit of a nightmare. And yet here you are, all jolly and bucolic!"

"I'm sorry about sounding so gloomy," said Kate. "I did feel terribly strange at first, and things got worse and worse until I hit a sort of all-time low. But looking back, that seems to have been a different me."

"I'll say!" Her mother sounded almost piqued. "I was expecting to find you pale and strained, and look at you—dying to haul me around your smelly farmyard! I know the country has its points but I never thought you'd start taking it *seriously*!"

"I don't," protested Kate, feeling her sophistication to be in question. Then she added, "But the farmyard isn't smelly. It's littered every day with nice fresh barley straw."

"Nice fresh barley straw!" repeated Nancy gloomily. "May the Lord deliver us. I'll go and see if Nigel wants some coffee."

The cold weather showed no sign of relenting, and when an afternoon's wintry sunshine melted the ice, it froze hard again overnight. The northeast wind persisted, bringing intermittent scatterings of knobbly snow.

"What on earth am I going to wear?" Kate lamented one evening. "I thought by the time I was getting bigger spring would be here and I could blossom into smocks and things. But it's still so beastly cold, and my jeans just won't do up. Not even with a safety pin."

"When Jane had Graham," said Beth, "she made a couple of tops that were like smocks without sleeves so she could wear woollies underneath. And trousers with strechy tops."

"That sounds marvelous," said Kate, "and not too difficult either. I used to make lots of clothes on

Mum's machine." But all that had stopped when she met Laurie. Laurie hadn't owned a sewing machine, and he would have thought dressmaking a ludicrous occupation. Kate brought her mind back to the present. "Is Jane your daughter? I ought to know all about the family, but I'm afraid I don't."

"Yes, Jane's the eldest," said Beth. "She live in Derbyshire, married a farmer. Then there's Michael, he's an engineer. Went off to Canada. And David. He's the clever one. Doing research at London University, something to do with organic chemistry. He come to see me sometimes. But stretchy trousers are the thing. Very comfy, Jane said."

"Have you got a sewing machine?" asked Kate.

"Oh, yes. The old treadle machine work as good as new. Jack wanted to buy me an electric one, but I didn't see the point. There's a little room upstairs I use for sewing—or used to. I'll show you."

Kate followed Beth upstairs, expecting to find a dusty attic with an antique machine shrouded in cobwebs.

"Here we are," said Beth, opening a door.

"Oh!" gasped Kate.

A built-in bench ran the length of the wall, and the treadle machine formed the center part of it. Drawers under the bench, Beth showed her, contained pins, scissors, paper patterns, and an immense variety of tapes and cotton and silk thread. A Victorian dressmaker's dummy stood primly naked and headless, its biscuit-brown calico awaiting the pins of the next creation. There was a comfortable swivel chair, an ironing board, and a plastic-topped table big enough to cut out on. And, to crown it all, the room was lit by modern, adjustable spotlights.

"I can't get over it!" Kate's astonishment made her feel quite short of breath. "I mean, here, in a farmhouse, a professional sewing room like this!"

"Jane used to teach needlework," explained Beth. "I never thought to show you before, not knowing you sewed."

"Did she build all this then—the drawers and everything?"

"Oh, no, Jack did that. He was so pleased when she went to college, he asked her what she wanted and just did it. He was very practical. Neither of us ever thought we'd have clever children, you see."

"I don't see why not," said Kate. "But can I really use this lovely room?"

"Of course you can. It's market day in Hadham tomorrow. That's the place to buy materials."

"And it's my clinic day on Thursday," Kate reminded her. "If you don't want to go into town two days running, perhaps I could leave it until Thursday and get some material then."

"Market stalls are much cheaper," said her aunt firmly. "And anyway, I want to see about some electric fencing, and the people are only there on cattle market day. If you want to look through those patterns, you might find something you can use."

Kate spent the rest of the evening delving about in her new found treasure room, and the next morning she accompanied her aunt to Hadham, happily clutching the paper patterns that Jane must have used to make the garments Beth had described.

The market stalls proved to be a fruitful hunting ground. Kate bought a soft, knitted wool fabric to make into trousers, black to go with everything, and a length of tweedy stuff in faint blue-gray checks for more practical use. She chose poplin for a top, the same blue as the tweed, and a couple of lengths of printed cotton. And, from a shop with a closing-down sale, she bought a blouse length of soft lawn printed in warm colors, rose, russet, terracotta, and purple. She showed this to Beth along with her other purchases when they got home and noticed with satisfaction that Beth picked it out as the one she liked best. Among the paper patterns in the sewing room Kate had found one in a larger size than the others. It was for a classic shirt-blouse, and along the top of it was written, "Mum. Cream shantung, pin-tucked."

If Jane could make a blouse for Beth, then, so, thought Kate, could she.

9

That afternoon Kate busied herself in the dressmaking room. She cut out the first pair of trousers, fitted them and sewed the main seams, and pinned the leg-end hems for hand stitching. By chicken-feeding time she had only the elasticized top section to make. She came down feeling very pleased with herself. Beth was already out on the afternoon feeding routine.

Kate fed the poultry, happy to notice that the drinkers were not frozen tonight. The grip of winter was at last relaxing, although the slick of water over the ice made the yards lethally slippery. She collected the eggs from the nest boxes in a plastic bucket and carried it with immense care back to the house. There she put the eggs onto trays, sorting brown from white. Then she mixed the milk for the lambs and funneled it into their bottles. She went into their shed and began to feed them.

Suddenly running footsteps approached, and Peter flung the shed door open.

"Kate, do you know where there's a blanket? Your aunt's had a fall in the cattle yard, and I think she's hit her head. She seem a bit groggy."

"Oh, Lord!" Kate dumped bottles and lambs and rushed indoors. Coming back with the blanket, she found Peter completing her job of feeding the lambs and wondered at his calm practicality.

"Thanks," he said, taking the blanket. "Ring Dr. McTaggart, will you? Number's in the book." And he was gone again.

Dr. McTaggart did not waste words either. "I'll come at once," he said, and hung up.

Kate went out, dreading what she might find. To her immense relief, she could hear her aunt's voice, raised in argument with Peter. Rounding the corner of the Dutch barn, she came upon an almost comic sight. Her aunt was sitting on the ground beside the gate into the bullock yard, struggling protestingly with the blanket that Peter was trying to pull over her. Behind the tubular steel gate, an audience of young Hereford bullocks stared inquisitively, their white faces adding a slightly surrealist touch to the scene.

"Just help me up," Beth was saying. "I'm quite all right. It's just my knee's a bit stiff."

"Which knee?" asked Kate, kneeling beside her on the wet, flinty surface of the yard.

"This one."

There was a ragged tear across the trouser leg, but

the dark material made it difficult to see any injury, especially as the daylight had almost gone and there was only a single bulb high up in the rafters. Looking at Beth's face, Kate saw with alarm that there was a large swelling above her left eye, dented across the middle with a dull red mark.

"I think we best get you indoors," said Peter.

"I'll just feed the bullocks," argued Beth. "Where's my bucket? I had it just now."

"I'll do those," said Peter. "I been feeding them every day since lambing, haven't I?"

"But I was going to do them tonight," said Beth. "Where *is* my bucket?"

Peter caught Kate's eye with a slight shake of his head as if to warn her against any argument. "Kate's got your bucket," he said. "Come along now." And, with a grunt of effort, he picked Beth up, blanket and all, and set off toward the house.

"I'm too heavy," Beth protested. Peter, Kate realized, had no breath to spare for a reply. She went ahead of him as quickly as she could across the slippery yard and opened the back door. Peter carried Beth in and put her down on the settee by the fire.

"Mustn't sit about like this," said Beth. Her face was very white, and the swelling on her head looked bigger than ever.

"Let's have these Wellies off," said Kate, tugging. With boots removed, it was easier to pull the trouser leg up over the injured knee. Kate's heart gave a lurch as she saw the mass of blood that soaked through the material and still welled from a deep gash.

"Best put a newspaper under that," said Peter. "She won't want a mess on her sofa."

Kate slipped the *East Anglian Daily Times* under the leg and said cheerily, "Don't worry. It's yesterday's!" Beth seemed about to make some response when her eyelids flickered strangely and she lost consciousness.

"Mind," said Peter, pushing Kate out of the way. He pulled Beth across to the edge of the settee so that her head was down. He knelt beside her, his weather-beaten face furrowed with anxiety. "Done too much for years," he said angrily, glaring at Kate as if it all had to be *somebody's* fault. "She's that obstinate." He peered anxiously into Beth's face, stroking a wisp of hair back from her unseeing eyes with clumsy, gentle fingers. "Come on, my beauty. Come on. It's all right." Beth made no move. "I'd have married her, you know," Peter said to Kate, not taking his eyes off Beth's face. "I always loved her. I'd have married her when Jack died, but I couldn't ask her then." He spoke in an agony of helplessness.

Beth moved a little but did not open her eyes, and Kate was immensely glad to see a car's headlights sweep across the window. "That's the doctor," she said, jumping up.

When Kate came back into the room with Dr. McTaggart, Beth had recovered consciousness, her head pillowed against Peter's arm. The waxy whiteness of her face was so unfamiliar that Kate felt frightened.

"And what have you been doing, Beth Kennett?" demanded the doctor. "Winter sports? Can we have a bowl of warm water, please, Kate?"

As he cleaned and swabbed, Kate felt apologetic. "I'd have done that," she said, "but there wasn't much time. She passed out, you see."

"Did she now." Dr. McTaggart was investigating the wound on the knee, which looked less alarming now that it was clean. "We'll have to X ray that. You may have cracked the patella. Now what about this goose egg you've grown on your head?" He examined the discolored swelling, feeling all around it carefully and shining a light into Beth's eyes.

"I must feed those bullocks," said Beth suddenly. She began to struggle up, but Dr. McTaggart gently overpowered her.

"They're fine," he insisted.

"They're not. Where are my boots?"

"Listen," said Kate, "Peter's *fed* the bullocks. They're *all right*."

"So don't you worry," agreed Peter in support of Kate's necessary lie. He glanced at his watch, and she knew the cattle would in truth be fed as soon as he could manage it.

"Now, Beth," said Dr. McTaggart, "I want you in hospital for a wee while. I'm going to ring for an ambulance, and I'll have no argument from you about it. Kate, come and show me where the phone is."

He led the way into the office and closed the door behind Kate.

"The phone's on the desk," said Kate.

"I know," agreed the doctor, "but I wanted a word with you. To start with, don't worry. The leg's not too bad, but she's a bit concussed, and that's why I want her in tonight, so she can be checked every hour or so. And don't tell me you could do it, because you can't. It's a specialized job. How are you feeling, anyway?"

"Oh, fine. Much better. I mean, better about being here." Kate, flustered by the accident, was getting muddled, but Dr. McTaggart seemed to understand.

"Good." He nodded. "I'm glad. Now look, can you put a few things together for your auntie? Toothbrush, dressing gown– You know the sort of thing."

Kate nodded and said, "I'll see if I can find a case."

Dr. McTaggart lifted the receiver and started to dial, and Kate went back through the kitchen on her way to the stairs. Beth was leaning comfortably against Peter, and neither of them seemed to notice Kate as she crossed the room.

In Beth's bedroom she felt like an intruder. Everything was very tidy, the drawers and cupboards closed, and the bed impeccably made. Despite Beth's practicality, it was a feminine room very much like Kate's own except that the carpet and curtains were a rich, rosy pink. She picked up a book from the bedside table and a pair of glasses in a case, but she felt reluctant to start hunting through the closed drawers. Beth's dressing gown hung on the back of the door so Kate put that over her arm and went downstairs again. Perhaps her aunt would be recovered enough to tell her where things were.

Beth looked up as Kate came in. She was still very pale and her left eye was closed by the enormous swelling over it, but she said, "There's a case ready packed in the bathroom cupboard."

"Oh, Beth," said Kate, "you are marvelous."

"I got caught out once before with nothing ready," said Beth. "Didn't I, Doctor?"

"You did indeed," agreed Dr. McTaggart. "But it's not so serious this time. You'll be out in a day or two."

"I'll be out tomorow morning," said Beth. "Soon as you've done your X rays."

"You'll do what you're told," said Peter severely. "No need to worry about things here. Kate and I can manage."

Far from being comforted by this assurance, Beth seemed confused and unhappy.

"Here's the ambulance," said Peter. And once again Kate was relieved to see headlights sweep into the yard.

Kate got up at six the next morning, knowing that

Beth usually started her day's work at this hour. Early as it was, though, the light was on in the lambing yard and Kate knew that Peter must be out there already. She put the kettle on and went out into the darkness. Old Glyn, unusually, trotted ahead of her across the slushy yard.

Peter was forking hay into the racks. "She's not here, boy," he said to the inquiring dog.

"I could have done that," said Kate, indicating the hay. "I'm quite used to helping. And I know you've got heaps to do out in the fields."

Peter finished his task. Then he stood the fork in the corner and said, "A girl in your condition got no right to be doing farm work. You can do your poultry if you're used to it, but I'll do the rest."

"But, Peter, it's—"

"I wouldn't mind a cup of tea," said Peter overbearingly, "and you could put some food out for the cats. They need a bit, this weather." He switched the light out, plunging them both into darkness, then led the way back to the house, Kate following his torch beam disconsolately. She felt rejected.

In the kitchen, Glyn flopped down on the hearthrug, and Peter, bootless, warmed his feet by the Aga. Kate made tea in silence.

"You don't want to be offended at what I said," remarked Peter. "There's plenty for you to do. Feed the lambs. You know how to make up the milk powder?"

"Yes," said Kate, still a little ruffled, "I've been doing it for ages."

"I've milked the cow," went on Peter. "The milk's in a bucket in the dairy. You can filter it, can't you?"

"Yes, and I'll feed yesterday's to the pigs," said Kate. She sighed irritably. "I do wish I could milk the cow."

Peter looked at her thoughtfully. "Now milking's a job a girl can do," he said. "I might teach you that."

"Oh, please!" Kate was eager.

"You're not a farmer's daughter for nothing then," said Peter with his slow smile.

"I don't know about that," said Kate. "It's just that I hate being left out of things. I want to *belong*. And you can't belong if you don't share in what's going on."

"Right enough," agreed Peter.

When he had drunk his tea and gone out, Kate completed her various tasks and went upstairs to make her bed. Outside it was just beginning to get light. Kate's breath misted on the window as she looked out. The sky was a deep, intense blue over the snowy fields, streaked with dramatic orange where the sun was near to rising. What a thing to try and paint, she thought. She must remember it carefully. It would be different later on. She had learned that the landscape shifted constantly in appearance, the balance of color and tone changing hour by hour as the light altered. In London things appeared dull or bright or wet according to the weather, but here the variations were much bigger.

Kate turned away from the window. This afternoon she had an appointment at the prenatal clinic, but Beth's accident would make it impossible for her to go. Drinking tea with Peter in the kitchen, though, had reminded her of another tea-drinking occasion when the miller and his son had been there. What were they called? Goodchild? Fairchild. That was it. Tom and Alec Fairchild. And Alec had said they might give her a lift if she needed it. Perhaps he hadn't meant it seriously, but it was worth a try. She went downstairs and looked up the number in Beth's address book, then dialed it. A woman answered.

"No, they're not in for breakfast yet," she answered. "You could ring again at about half-past eight. Or if you leave a message I'll pass it on."

Kate explained who she was and about Beth's accident. The woman clucked sympathetically. "Tom *will* be sorry to hear about that," she said. "It's Mrs. Fairchild here, by the way. I'll get Tom to ring you soon as he comes in."

"Thank you," said Kate, feeling that Mrs. Fairchild's offer was a definite advance on her first reaction. How valuable friends were, out here where nobody had close neighbors!

She rang up the hospital and asked after Beth, to be told that, "Mrs. Kennett is quite comfortable. Visiting hours are three to four and seven to eight, if you want to see her."

Good, thought Kate. She would visit Beth after her prenatal appointment, Fairchilds willing. The daylight was stronger now. Her hens would have wakened up. Kate went outside.

Mrs. Willisham cycled up with the morning paper and post while Kate was still busy with the poultry. She had met a night nurse from the hospital on her way around and had heard about Beth's accident but was agog for further details from Kate. The telephone, which rang a loud outside bell in the yard, released Kate from further gossip.

"Hello, Alec Fairchild here. Sorry to hear about Beth. I'm going into Hadham this afternoon. What time do you want to be there?"

"My appointment's at two o'clock."

"Pick you up twenty past one then?"

"That would be lovely. Visiting time is at three, so I thought I might pop in and see Beth. Would that be all right?"

"Do well. How is she?"

"They said quite comfortable."

"Never tell you much, do they? See you later then. 'Bye."

"Good-bye."

Kate replaced the receiver a little uneasily. Had she been a frightful nuisance? He sounded rather brisk, as if she had interrupted him in the middle of more important things. In that case, she decided, it was all the kinder of him to bother. She went into the kitchen and sorted the mail, which she had pushed into her parka pocket. There was a letter from Laurie.

Sweet Kate,
How wonderful you are—so fresh and immediate, almost to the point of clumsiness. Your letter touched me with its halting phrases about Barbara. Its very absence of sympathy made me realize what you had left unsaid. With all my heart I envy you. Life still comes fresh to you. Painting is a pleasure to you as blowing bubbles is a pleasure to a child, whereas for me it is hard, self-searching work. Perhaps that is why I love you. You are my touchstone, my magic contact with things natural. Little cat, you still walk alone and stare with green-gray eyes at all contrivance, smiling privately. Maddening little cat, you are never there when I need you. And when you are there, you elude me. Your quietness springs from a calm I cannot penetrate; your laughter troubles me. I am a buffoon, a puffed-up seeker after style. I say a lot, but it is about nothing. I cannot simply *be*. Barbara's funeral is on Tuesday. I do so wish you could be there, an island of sanity in what will, I know, be an ocean of distressing and absurd ritual. Is there any hope that you can come? I must see you soon, anyway, for we have so much to talk about. Write to me soon, little cat. Or better, ring me about the funeral so I know.
My love,
L.

Kate gave a shudder at the thought of Barbara's funeral. Thank goodness she could not go and had a cast-iron reason for staying here. For a guilty moment she was almost glad that Beth was in hospital. She pushed the letter back into its envelope. That could wait until later. It was more important to try and finish those maternity trousers in time for this afternoon.

10

For the first mile or two in the bouncy Land-Rover Alec Fairchild talked about Beth. He admired her for the way she had run the farm since Jack died. "But there'll come a time," he said, "when she can't keep on. I don't know what she'll do then."

"Neither do I," said Kate. "It's her whole life. She never even takes a holiday." She felt a little shy of Alec. He was so assured, so completely a part of the farming community that, by contrast, she seemed an outsider again.

There was silence for a while, and then Alec asked, "Are you going back to London after the baby's born?"

"I don't know," said Kate rather miserably. His question intensified her sense of not belonging. "Things are in rather a muddle. I thought I was going to marry Laurie. That's the baby's father. But the longer I'm away, the more I don't want to." She gave a little laugh. "Silly, isn't it?"

Alec's answering smile was an absentminded response. After a while he said, "If you've been here this long, at this bad time of the year, and still find you like it, then I don't reckon you'll settle back in London. There's farming in the family, you see."

"That's almost what Peter said," remarked Kate.

"He's a good old boy, Peter. He'd do anything for Beth, you know. Worships the ground she walks on."

"I know. He told me last night. Beth had passed out and—" Kate could not go on. Remembering Peter's clumsy hands touching Beth's face so gently, she was unbearably moved. She tried again. "He was lovely." She stared out across the fields, fighting for self-control. Things weren't too good today. Her early start had resulted in a feeling of shivery tiredness, and the maternity trousers felt bulky and unfamiliar. Perhaps they would be better when she had made a smock to go with them, but at present she missed her comfortable but impossible old jeans, and for the first time she felt embarrassed by the bulge that was making everything so awkward. There was something else, too. The presence of Alec beside her was a vivid reminder of the male companionship she no longer had. Although Laurie was not always a very sympathetic person, he could be relied on to give her a hug and a kiss if she was feeling despondent. There was something undermining about physical loneliness. Peter Thurlow loved Beth. But who loved Kate? Nobody.

Kate clenched her hands tightly together in her lap. She mustn't cry here.

Alec glanced at her curiously. "Hey," he said. "What's the matter?" He swung the Land-Rover into a gateway and stopped. Then he put his arm around Kate's shoulders and gave her a gentle hug and a shake. She turned to him blindly, buried her face in the tweedy roughness of his jacket, and wept.

With his free hand, Alec switched off the engine and fished for a box of Kleenex. "Here," he said, when Kate had recovered a little. "Blow."

Kate blew, ashamed of herself, and yet feeling much comforted. "I'm awfully sorry," she said. "I'm not usually so stupid."

"It's not stupid," Alec assured her. "It must be pretty lonely out there, and Beth's accident was more of a shock than you thought. Women are always weepy when they're pregnant, anyway. My sister's terrible. She says it comes over her that she needs a hug, and that's that!"

Kate nodded, with a rather watery smile.

"Our vet's got some nutty theory about spinal fluid," Alec went on. "He says it's actually good for animals to be stroked. And we're all animals, when you come right down to it." He restarted the engine. "Better get going or you'll be late. All right now?"

"Yes, thank you." Kate still felt rather tremulous and thought she had better keep talking. "How many children has your sister got?"

"Four," said Alec, looking over his shoulder to see that the lane was clear. He pulled out. "That's my eldest sister, Ellen. She's twenty-seven, five years older than me. But there's two other girls between, Deb and Liza. I'm the baby of the family."

"I do hope it's not putting you out, giving me a lift," said Kate. "You sounded rather busy this morning."

Alec laughed. "That was Mum's fault. She said, 'Now you're to be *nice* to that girl, Alec. You're not to sound cheeky and familiar.' So with her listening, I didn't know *what* to say."

"Does she know about–"

"The baby? Oh, yes, of course she does. Everyone knows about that. That's why she was making sure I behaved myself."

"Why?"

"Well, it's obvious to her that you've been badly treated by some utter cad. She's very old-fashioned, is Mum. So I'm to be the Perfect Gentleman. Which I am!"

Kate gave a contented little sigh. "Lovely." Things being what they were, she thought, a perfect gentleman was exactly what she needed.

A welcoming hand waved from among the sea of dumpy figures in the waiting room, and Kate recognized Tessa Cooney, the girl she had talked to last time. She went over and sat beside her. Tessa's bulge looked very much bigger.

"Hello!" she greeted Kate enthusiastically. "I say, isn't your husband good-looking!"

Kate was totally thrown. "My husband?"

"Yes, Laurie, he's called, isn't he? I was looking out of the window and saw you get out of the Land-Rover. Talk about tall, dark, and handsome, and the lovely courteous way he helped you down! I do like a man with good manners!"

"Actually, that isn't Laurie, I'm afraid. That's—a sort of neighbor. He was coming into town so he gave me a lift."

"Do forgive me, Kate." Tessa seemed embarrassed. "What a stupid mistake. But I'm sure Laurie's just as gorgeous!"

Kate smiled. She thought of Laurie's long, wispy, fair hair and rather cadaverous face and could hardly describe him as gorgeous. And once again she had allowed the fictional husband to go unchallenged and made it more difficult to disentangle the truth.

"When are you due?" she asked, getting onto safer ground.

"April the fifth, just over three weeks. I thought I was going to have a spring baby, but it's still awfully wintry, isn't it?"

"Perishing," agreed Kate. "That's why I'm still wearing trousers. The nurse made an awful fuss, but I only need a few seconds to take them off."

"You've got more strength of character than me,"

said Tessa, glancing ruefully at her bare white legs. "Not that it's cold in here."

"I don't care," said Kate. "It's the principle of the thing."

Dr. McTaggart walked briskly past the lines of chairs, clipboard in hand. "Kate!" he exclaimed, when he saw her. "You'll be wanting to visit your auntie. Come along, my dear, you can jump the queue for once. She's feeling much better today, but we'll keep an eye on her a wee while longer."

"My word," said Tessa, as Kate got up, "you *are* a lucky girl today!"

She spoke, Kate thought, with just a trace of irony.

"Hello," said Beth. "I didn't think I'd be seeing you." The lump on her forehead was not quite as big, but a dark patch of bruising had spread outward to engulf her eye, which was closed and very swollen.

"Mr. Fairchild gave me a lift."

"Good old Tom. That was nice of him."

"No, it was Alec. Mrs. Fairchild said she'd tell Tom when I rang up, but Alec was the one who phoned."

"Oh." Beth's open eye looked thoughtful, but all she said was, "Do just as well."

"How are you, anyway? You gave us an awful fright last night."

"Not so bad. They've sewn my knee up, and I haven't broken anything. What a night, though. I'd just get to sleep, and they'd come and shine a light in my eyes and ask a lot of silly questions. I'd have been better at home in my own bed."

"When are they letting you out?"

"Tomorrow, I think." Beth closed her good eye for a few moments. "I've got an awful headache," she said.

"I bet you have," said Kate.

The swing doors at the end of the ward opened, and Alec came in, looking immensely healthy by contrast with the listless patients. Tessa was quite right, Kate thought as she watched him walk down the ward. With his blue eyes and wide mouth and curly brown hair, he really was a very handsome young man. She felt quite maternal in being able to say so objectively, having no interest herself in his attributes. It was strange how pregnancy set one apart, she thought. Arriving, Alec smiled down at Beth.

"Been bullfighting again, have you?"

"That's it." Beth smiled back, responding to his liveliness. A nurse scuttled up and touched Kate's arm.

"If your husband would like to sit down, dear, there's some chairs by the door."

Oh, dear. Two mistakes in one afternoon. Kate blushed, but Alec smiled cheerfully at the nurse and said, "Thanks. I'll go and get one."

"There you are," said Beth with a grin. "You've got yourself a husband."

"How awful for him," said Kate, still red-faced. "I do wish people wouldn't jump to conclusions." When Alec came back with the chair, she avoided meeting his eye and was grateful for the smooth way he took up the conversation, teasing Beth gently about her strenuous life. Quite soon, though, Beth began to look very tired and Alec sensibly got to his feet and said he would have to be going.

"Yes," agreed Kate, "me, too, or the hens will go to sleep without their supper."

" 'Spect I'll be home tomorrow," said Beth.

But her hands lay slack on the white sheet, and Kate said, "There's no hurry. Get all the rest you can, while you've got the chance. Oh, Peter says he'll come and see you this evening."

Walking along the stone corridor with Alec when they had left the ward, she felt that she had to apologize for the embarrassing mistake she had caused.

"I'm sorry about that," she said. "Stupid nurse."

"What, taking me for your better half, you mean? Oh, don't worry about that. I think it's rather a laugh."

"Yes," agreed Kate with only a trace of hesitation, "I suppose it is, really."

He held the door open for her, and she went out into the raw cold of the parking lot. As he unlocked the Land-Rover Alec looked at the sky and said, "The wind's changed. Thank goodness for that. We should get some spring weather now."

* * *

Spring did, indeed, come rapidly in the next few days. By the time Beth arrived home, the snow had disappeared completely, revealing ready-blooming crocuses and the thick shoots of daffodil bulbs. Blackthorn blossomed in the hedges, and Kate found three goose eggs buried in the straw, huge white things too big for her fingers to close around. She carried them into the kitchen and showed them to Beth, who was making bread at the table, perched on a stool to take the weight off her leg.

"About time, too," she said, nodding at the eggs. "They're late starting this year. The cold weather put them off. When there's a few more, we'll start the incubator."

So Kate soon found herself with another job to do, keeping the incubator supplied with paraffin and making sure it stayed at a constant temperature of 104 degrees Fahrenheit, and that its water trays were full. Greasy-shelled duck eggs were put in it as well as the goose eggs, and they all had to be turned each morning and evening and sprinkled with a little water.

"It seems ages to wait," she said, as she turned the silent, unpromising eggs one evening.

"Only twenty-eight days," Beth reproved her. "That's not long. And you needn't turn them for the last week."

Sure enough, one morning in mid-April when Kate

went to look at the eggs, she heard chirping. Fascinated, she picked up an egg with a little splintering hole beginning to appear in its shell and listened to it. A loud, peremptory chirping came from inside it, and a renewed attack from the tiny, energetic beak enlarged the escape hole. A few hours later the duckling was out, wet and stringy-looking but open-eyed and full of energy. The next morning there were twenty-three ducklings among a litter of eggshell debris, and seven long-necked goslings covered with hairy gray-and-yellow fluff. Kate put them into the brooder, a contraption shaped like a very squat trash can with a burner in the middle protected with perforated metal, and, on Beth's instructions, fed them with chopped hard-boiled egg. She was acutely reminded of the Silver Snack Bar as she shelled the eggs, and she felt a strong residue of nausea as the smell of them reached her nose. The fresh eggs from her own hens, though, were somehow far less offensive than the ones she had dealt with in the snack bar, and her aversion to them was more than compensated for by her pleasure in watching the little birds shovel up the white and yellow crumbs.

"What are we going to do about the turkey?" she asked one day. "She hasn't got a mate."

"We must get a gobbler," agreed Beth. "I had one. Saved the pair of them to breed this year. The others went for Christmas. But the gobbler got bronchitis just before you came, and I found him dead in the yard. We'll get her a mate soon; then her eggs will be fertile. She's not laying yet, is she?"

"I don't think so," said Kate. "What do turkey eggs look like?"

"A bit bigger than duck-sized," said Beth. "Pointed, and speckled with brown."

"Then she isn't," said Kate.

The bantams had started to go broody, and Kate knew now how to recognize the difference between a laying bird and a sitting one. A broody hen had a preoccupied look in her eye, and when touched she ruffled up her feathers with a shivering, irritated *Brrr* noise, followed by a series of maternal clucks as she rearranged her eggs under her feathers.

Kate spoke of the poultry in her letters to Laurie and to her mother, but neither of them responded with more than amusement to her new interests. Laurie had not written much since Barbara died. Kate's refusal to come to the funeral had provoked a furious letter expressing deep hurt at being put second to "your bleating, snorting, cackling brutes, which any lout could adequately guard." Kate had been offended and since then had refrained from offering any news about the farm, which left her very little to write about.

Her days were increasingly busy. She made clothes for herself and the baby and made up the blouse for Beth from the material she had bought in the market.

Beth was delighted with it and said, "I'll save that for when I want to look really smart." Encouraged, Kate decided to make herself a dress to wear after the baby was born. Something "really smart." Something to look forward to. Meanwhile, she helped Beth with the spring planting in the garden and went into Hadham for further prenatal appointments. She went also to relaxation classes where she learned exactly how childbirth worked and how to help the natural process along by controlling her muscles and her breathing. On these occasions Alec again was the one who gave her a lift in the Land-Rover. Beth's leg had been stiff and painful since her accident, and she found driving uncomfortable, and Peter was using every minute of the daylight to get ahead with planting his spring wheat and barley.

The spring weather made Kate feel much happier, and in a while she found herself more at ease with Alec. He never referred to her emotional breakdown on the first dreadful day after Beth's accident, not, Kate thought, because he was being tactful but simply because it had not mattered to him. She enjoyed his company very much. He had an amused, optimistic outlook that softened his tough practicality. He found people funny and encouraged Kate not to let things matter too much. Like Beth, he was impatient with "fuss." When he came to collect her one day, his left hand was heavily bandaged. "Caught it on a bit of barbed wire," he said. "Silly twit." Only later, when she saw the half-healed tear that ran right across his palm, did she realize how severe the injury had been. She began to look forward to seeing him. Although she had become very fond of Beth, her aunt belonged to an older generation. Alec, with his abundant energy and good humor, was sheer fun, despite his rather Puritanical respect for hard work.

"You must come to Young Farmers with me when you've had this baby," he said once. "You'll meet lots of people there."

Kate shrank a little. She had come to trust Alec, but the thought of the Young Farmers' Club was frightening. They would be tough, efficient people full of jokes she would not understand. She deflected the suggestion, laughing. "*When* I've had this baby!" she said. "It's beginning to seem like the Beatles song, 'When I'm Sixty-four!' "

But in fact the baby was becoming more and more real to Kate. One day as spring began to give way to summer she felt a flutter of movement inside her, and in the next few days its separate, energetic life became quite distinct.

In between her other activities, Kate continued to make good use of the art materials her friends had sent her. She drew and painted all the things that interested her, from the pattern of the clouds in the sky to the flyaway shapes of the washing blowing on the line. Strangely, the more she drew, the more there was to look at. She was fascinated by the silky ripple of sea-green young wheat in the field, but equally, she would linger in the vegetable garden, examining the clutching tendrils of peas and staring at the fleshy squash plants, fingering their hollow stalks and floppy yellow flowers.

Beth thought Kate's pictures were beautiful. "I like the way you've got it all in," she said. "A bit higgledy-piggledy, but it's there. You've even put the sheep under the apple trees." The ewes and lambs had been turned to graze in the orchard, but Kate's bottle-fed lambs, although long weaned, still ran bleating to the fence when they saw her.

A card arrived from Tessa, forwarded from the hospital. It had a picture of a stork on the front and inside announced the birth of Sophia Jane Cooney, 7 lbs 6 oz. Kate felt happy for Tessa, but at the same time she was relieved to know that she would not meet her again at the prenatal clinic. Kate hated the deception that had arisen, and yet she lacked the courage to destroy it. Although she was almost certain that Tessa would not mind, she still shrank from the moment of telling her.

Beth's son, David ("the clever one," Kate remembered), came to stay for a weekend late in May. He had inherited Beth's florid complexion but was otherwise unlike her. He talked a lot, expressing intelligent and well-informed views about what was going on in the world. Beth, obviously proud of him, was content to listen. She showed him some of Kate's paintings, and, to Kate's surprise, he looked at them with close interest.

"You could sell these," he said. "Frame them nicely and get them to a London gallery, and they'd go like hot cakes. People are mad about this primitive stuff these days. You're a second Grandma Moses, my dear."

Kate had no idea what he was talking about. She felt a little suspicious of David. Although he was very nice to her, she felt that he regarded her as a joke, one of his mother's eccentricities. And on Sunday morning as she came into the office from feeding the hens she heard him ask his mother in the kitchen, "Where's your stray cat this morning? Gone to chase her chickens?" She only caught the reproving tone of Beth's reply, but there was no doubt what David meant. The descriptions stung, and it reminded her afresh that she did not belong here. She was indeed a stray cat that had found a comfortable place in which to kitten and afterward– Kate shook her head. There was no need to dwell on that. Beth had said to her once, "I reckon more than half of any misery is self-pity. And you can do without that." It was a tough piece of advice, but one that Kate had found to be true.

11

One day on the way to Hadham in the Land-Rover Alec said, "It's time you learned to drive."

"Yes."

Kate was instantly worried. She had begun to take it for granted that Alec would give her a lift when she needed it, assuming that he had to go into Hadham for business reasons. He had always assured her that he was going to the bank, or had to see someone about an order, or was going through the town on his way to another farm; but perhaps in fact he was finding her presence a nuisance. Obviously it must be a time-consuming duty to pick her up from Willow Farm and perhaps wait about for her in Hadham until she came out of the hospital. Beth was beginning to drive now. Perhaps Kate would not have to bother Alec so much in the future. But it would be better not to bother Beth either.

"I ought to have got something organized," she said, frowning.

"And just what were you going to organize?"

"Well—find a driving school, I suppose, and fix some lessons."

"Don't be daft," said Alec. "If you've got enough money for expensive driving lessons, you'd be better to spend it on buying a car. Then you'll have transport of your own."

Kate felt confused. "But until I've had some lessons I couldn't drive it."

"*I'll* teach you to drive, you great twit!" said Alec. "Unless you'd *rather* go to a driving school, that is."

"Oh, no, of course I wouldn't! Are you sure, though? Won't it take up an awful lot of your time?"

"Of course I'm sure. I wouldn't offer otherwise, would I? Things aren't too bad now until harvest. You won't see much of me then."

Kate thought. She still had the money Laurie had given her, intact in its paper wrappings. He had not referred to it in any of his letters, but Kate regarded it as a loan rather than a gift, although his first letter had spoken of "my gift to you." Aloud, she said, "I could always sell a car again when I go back to London, couldn't I?"

"I suppose so," said Alec rather crossly. Kate knew that he disliked any reference to her return to London, but she felt that she must not be lulled into any dream world. She had to keep her feet on the ground. "I've got three hundred pounds," she told him. "Laurie gave it to me in case I changed my mind and wanted an abortion. So I don't think of it as permanently mine, you see."

"Good God!" Alec was scandalized. "You *wouldn't* have had an abortion, would you?"

"No. That's what all the trouble was about. I always wanted the baby."

"I should think so, too, poor little beggar."

Kate laughed. "Anyone would think it was yours!"

"Well," said Alec crossly, "after all this time, I feel I've got a fatherly interest in it. What about this car then? You could sell it again, as you say. Do you want me to keep an ear to the ground?"

"Yes," said Kate recklessly, "why not?"

Alec rang the very next morning with news of a car.

"How do you fancy a Morris Minor Traveller?"

"A what?"

"One of those little station wagons with wooden coachwork and windows all around. Look a bit like a traveling cottage." Kate liked Alec's occasional lapse into Suffolk speech. It made him seem less cool and efficient.

"How much would it cost?"

"He wanted three fifty but he'll take three hundred if you've got pound notes."

"Oh, yes," said Kate, dazed, "I've got pound notes."

Beth, having overheard, gave Kate an amused glance as she went into the kitchen. "What have you been up to?"

"I seem to have bought a car," said Kate. And she told Beth all about it.

"Well," said Beth at the end of the recital, "I don't know what your Laurie's going to say, but there's no denying that's useful, being able to drive, wherever you are."

"Anyway," Kate said, "Alec's bringing it over this afternoon. He's got to collect some stuff from the vet, so he'll go in my little car and bring it here on the way back. If you're OK to give him a lift home, that is."

"Yes, I don't mind that," said Beth.

The Traveller turned out to be pale blue between its timber parts and rather rusty, but Kate loved it at once.

"It's *sweet*!" she said. "And there's so much room in it!"

"There's a back seat fold up if you want it," Alec pointed out. "But when it's down the way it is now, that give you plenty of room for a car crib."

"Oh, yes!" Kate blushed with added delight, forgetting that in London the parking was so scarce and expensive that she was unlikely to drive anything larger than a baby carriage, even if Laurie didn't want his money back. "I do wish I had a license and learner plates and everything. Then I could start straight away!"

"You can," said Alec. "As long as it's on private property you don't need anything official." He opened the driver's door. "In you get."

Kate panicked. "I can't! Not right now. Let me get used to the idea first."

"Rubbish," said Alec. "Don't worry. You're not going to drive it. Not today. Just sit in it, and I'll show you the controls."

This sounded harmless enough. Kate sat in the driving seat. "The pedals are rather a long way away," she said.

"You want the seat a bit closer," said Alec. "The last owner was taller than you."

"Your cowman had a car like that, Alec," said Beth. "Ernie Chapman."

"It is Ernie Chapman's," said Alec. "I know he's always looked after it, and if Kate wants to sell it any time, I'd be willing to buy it off her for what she gave him. Good little car."

"Oh, Alec!" Kate was touched. "Would you really?"

"You keep asking me if I mean things," said Alec tetchily, but trying not to grin. "Of course I do!"

"Talk about having your cake and eating it!" remarked Beth. "Well, I'll leave you to your lesson." And she went off across the yard.

"She does limp these days," said Kate, watching her go.

"I'm afraid she does, poor old girl," agreed Alec. "Now this pedal on the left is the clutch."

* * *

True to his promise, Alec did not let Kate drive the car on the first day, but he came often to the farm in the following weeks, and when Kate had overcome her nervousness, she found the little car quite easy to manage. There was plenty of room around the farm where she could practice turning and reversing, and she learned more quickly on her own than she did with Alec sitting beside her. Beth refused to be impressed by her progress. "That always seem easy at first," she said. "That's not the same thing when you're out on the road, though. Driving's a funny business. Take a long time to be good at it."

Kate found this to be true. When she had her learner plates and ventured onto public roads, her coordination would sometimes desert her and she felt as frightened and flustered as she had been at first sight of the car. One afternoon in a narrow lane a tractor pulled out of a farm gateway right in front of the Traveller. "Brake!" shouted Alec. Kate's foot was already hard down, but she forgot about the clutch and stalled the engine, sending the car into a sideways skid on the sandy surface of the lane. It hurtled hard into the hedge, where it stopped.

"Turn your ignition," said Alec with unshakable calm. "Hand brake on. Are you all right?"

"Yes," said Kate breathlessly. "I'm awfully sorry."

"Not your fault," said Alec. "Wait here a minute."

He got out of the car and went down the lane toward the tractor driver, who had stopped and was coming back on foot to see if any damage had been caused. Alec grabbed the man by the front of his overalls and shook him. Then, fists clenched, he said a few words to him and walked back to the car.

"One of our men," he said, getting in. "Stupid bugger."

"I thought you were going to kill him!" said Kate. "Did you threaten to give him the sack or something?"

"Something is right," said Alec grimly. "I told him if he ever did that again I'd knock his teeth down his throat. Now check that you're in neutral and start the engine."

Kate did as she was told.

Peter Thurlow kept his promise to teach Kate to milk. "Don't be afraid of it," he said, crouched beside her as she sat by the cow. "You won't hurt her." Freda, the Guernsey cow, turned her long head to stare at her unaccustomed milker.

"If she blow at you, breathe back," instructed Peter. "She only want to know who you are."

Freda's breath smelled sweet and grassy, and she seemed to approve of Kate, for she turned back to her manger and resumed her munching.

"Take the top of the teat between your finger and thumb so you trap the milk, like this," instructed Peter.

"Then close your other fingers to squeeze it out, pulling down a bit. Always think, you're milking *down.* Some beginners seem to think they're milking *up.*"

Kate squeezed anxiously. A few drops of milk came out, but nothing like the easy flow that Peter could produce.

"Let down, you old bugger," he said to the cow, thumping her udder with a clenched fist.

"Doesn't that hurt her?"

"No," scoffed Peter. "Ha'n't you seen what a calf do? Bunt with his nose a lot harder than that."

Suddenly Kate could feel that there was milk in the teats. She squeezed out a thin jet with her right hand, another with her left. Right–left.

"It's awfully hard work," she said. "My hands feel so feeble."

"You get used to it," said Peter. He watched her for a while then said, "That'll do. I'll finish her off, or we'll run out of let-down time."

Kate made way for him, her hands and arms aching. The milk gushed through Peter's stubby fingers in foaming torrents, spurting into the mere inch she had managed to accumulate in the bottom of the bucket.

Never mind, Kate thought. I've made a start.

Beth's leg continued to improve, but she would not come out with Kate in the Traveller. "I'm sorry, my dear," she said firmly, "but I'm a bit of a nervous passenger." However, her lack of confidence in Kate was amply compensated for by Alec, who accompanied her on increasingly long drives and even allowed her to take the Traveller into Hadham.

On the way back from a hospital appointment one day, he said, "You'd better get an application in for your driving test. There's a bit of a waiting list."

"Do you think I'd pass?" asked Kate, surprised.

"Don't see why not."

But Kate was aware that her increasing size was soon going to make it difficult to fit herself into the driving seat. She explained this to Alec, adding gloomily, "I was an idiot, buying this car. I should have known I'd get too big to drive it. I suppose I did know, really, but I just didn't believe it. Nobody can *ever* have been as huge as I am."

"Rubbish," said Alec. "You should have seen my sister. Twice your size, every time. Anyway, it doesn't matter. If you get a date for your test in about mid-September, you'll be slim again after the baby and that'll give you time for a bit of practice if you've had to give up driving for a bit."

"But suppose I'm not here?" she said.

Alec frowned. "You won't be rushing off anywhere straight away," he said. "Not with a young baby."

"Perhaps not." Kate stared rather dismally along the road in front of her. "I feel as if I'm waiting for something to happen but I don't know what. Beth's been absolutely sweet, but I think she likes the place to herself, really. There's always Peter if she wants company. And anyway, I can't stay at the farm forever. I've got to make my own life."

"And where does this chap Laurence fit in?"

Kate laughed at Alec's obvious hostility. "Don't be so old-fashioned! It's not all his fault, you know!" But there was something nagging at the back of her mind about Laurie. Something she had to face. "Actually," she said, "he wrote the other day and said he'd like to come and see me to talk things over. He said he'd ring."

"Come *here*, d'you mean?"

"Well, yes. There's no reason why he shouldn't. It would just be a day's visit."

"He's got cheek," said Alec indignantly.

"I don't know. It would be rather nice to see him." Kate sprang to Laurie's defense, although she was secretly nervous about his arrival. He was so different from anybody here. And he was the person she had known, so long ago it seemed, in London, when she, too, had been a different person. What would he make of Beth, with her Suffolk speech and her red, ugly face? And what would Beth make of him? Perhaps Alec would be a helpful go-between, if he could be persuaded to be nice. At least he spoke BBC English, give or take the occasional lapse. "You must meet Laurie, Alec. He's a very amusing person."

"I don't reckon he'd amuse me," said Alec. Suffolk

people, Kate thought, were decidedly odd about strangers.

Laurie rang up that evening. "Kate, how are you fixed for a flying visit tomorrow? It's the only day I can come in the next three weeks. I'm starting a big new project with Hilary Billinghurst. You know that girl from Beeb graphics? Bags of ideas."

"As far as I'm concerned it's fine, but I'll have to check with Beth."

"Do that afterward, dear. No point in wasting phone time. Ring if it's no good, but otherwise I'll be coming."

"All right. Do you want meeting at the station?"

"You bet I do. I wouldn't get far otherwise! I'm getting up at absolute *crack* of dawn to catch the nine-fifteen from Liverpool Street. There's only about three trains a day to your frightful place, and they take hours. I think it arrives at about ten forty-five. Can you disentangle yourself that early?"

"Yes, that'll be fine."

"Anything you want from the great metropolis?"

Kate thought quickly. "I tell you what I *would* like —a point-o-four variant for my Rapidograph. I've got a three, but I really do want a slightly thicker one."

"I expect I've got a spare one. You're still drawing then?"

"Oh, yes, it keeps me amused for hours."

"Amused!" Laurie sighed. "That's what I mean about

you. No hard work, no responsibilities, just float along. Totally irresponsible."

"Oh, Laurie, I'm not!"

"Yes, you are," he insisted. "That's why I love you. See you tomorrow."

"At Coptoft Magna, ten forty-five."

"Coptoft Magna," repeated Laurie faintly. "My God, I must be mad. 'Bye."

Beth, when told of Laurie's plan, looked worried. "The vet's coming to do the blood tests. We're bringing all the cows and heifers in first thing, and then each one's got to go in the crush for him to take a blood sample. I'll be busy with that all morning. Can't leave it all to Peter. Any other day this week—"

"He can only come tomorrow," said Kate, with secret relief. "Never mind. I'll ring him and tell him to leave it for a bit."

"Can't Alec take you?" said Beth. "Or go with you in your car? Ring him up and see."

"He came into Hadham with me yesterday," objected Kate. "I can't *keep* asking him."

"You ring him up," insisted Beth.

Reluctantly Kate did so.

12

On the way to Coptoft Magna, Alec said, "Beth wants a turkey stag, doesn't she?"

"Yes, she does!" Kate responded with alacrity, for Alec had sat beside her in grumpy silence since they left Willow Farm.

"If you turn left about a mile from here, we can get one. I don't often come this way, or I'd have picked one up before."

"But it'll flap all around the car!"

"No, it won't. We'll put it in a sack."

"Will it be all right in a sack?"

"Of *course* it'll be all right," said Alec irritably. "But if you don't want one, it's no skin off my nose. It's not *my* turkey hen that's going to mope all summer."

Glancing at him rather nervously, Kate saw that Alec had the beginnings of a grin twitching at the corners of his mouth. He was never serious for very long.

"What are you up to?" she asked. "You look as if you're enjoying a private joke."

"Turn left here," said Alec.

Fred Langham's poultry farm was a babble of noise, and the noisiest birds of all were the turkeys.

"Morning, Fred!" shouted Alec above the din. "Have you got a nice bronze turkey stag for breeding? Not too heavy for the job, you know."

"Got just the thing," Fred shouted back.

He and Alec disappeared into one of the buildings and came out with an angry turkey tied in a soft burlap bran sack from which his red-wattled head and neck protruded. He was clearly furious. There was so much noise going on that Kate did not realize until they drove away just how much of it was being made by their particular turkey. His high-pitched rattling gobble was deafening, and his imprisoning sack lurched about alarmingly.

"Oh, dear," Kate shouted, "Laurie's not going to like this!"

Alec chuckled happily. "Should ha' stayed in London, bor!" he shouted back in richest Suffolk. And Kate, despite her fury with him, could not restrain a giggle at the thought of the ill-assorted carload she would have to drive back to Willow Farm.

Laurie was the only person to get off the London train. He was hatless, to Kate's relief (she had rather dreaded the checked cap), and wore an immense oiled wool sweater that had been knitted for some outsize member of a lifeboat crew. On Laurie, it reached almost to his knees. He carried an Army knapsack and looked small and vulnerable. Kate warmed to him with a strong resurgence of affection.

"Laurie!" She ran along the platform to meet him.

"Katie. Hello, pet." He gave her a hug and a kiss. "Who's the brawny peasant?" He indicated Alec, who was lounging against the waiting-room door, hands in pockets.

"Alec Fairchild. He's awfully nice. He's been teaching me to drive. He came with me this morning because Beth's hung up at the farm, doing blood tests."

Laurie shuddered.

"It's for brucellosis and TB," Kate explained. "It's only a routine thing. Laurie, I've bought a car! I had to use the money you lent me, but it's a sweet car and it'll be so useful, being able to drive—" Kate realized that she was prattling. "But how are you, anyway?"

"Exhausted," said Laurie promptly. They had reached Alec, and Kate introduced them.

"Morning," said Alec cheerfully, shaking Laurie's hand in a powerful grip.

"Steady," said Laurie, extricating himself. "I have no pretensions to manual strength. I never lift anything heavier than a pint beer mug if I can help it."

Alec grinned, disarmed by his candor. "Kate says you're an artist," he said.

"Of a sort," Laurie agreed. "You must be something agricultural, I take it?"

"We're farmers and millers, yes." Alec led the way down the steps to the parking lot.

"Gold miners, no less!" said Laurie.

"You townies don't want to believe all you're told," said Alec. "In you get, Kate, and try to keep it down to under eighty. He may be nervous." He ushered Laurie firmly into the back seat of the car and got in beside Kate. "As driving instructor," he said over his shoulder, "I think I ought to take the risk of sitting beside her."

There was an outburst of furious gobbling from the turkey, and Laurie jumped. "Christ!" he said. "What's that?"

"A turkey," said Kate calmly, and started the engine. Laurie did not seem so overpowering here. It was as though he had shrunk in relation to the large scale of the landscape. Or perhaps without his London background he seemed less impressive. Whatever it was, Kate felt that she was definitely in charge.

"Beth, this is Laurie Coppersmith. Laurie, this is my aunt, Beth Kennett."

"Hello."

"Hello, Laurie. Oh, Alec, you've bought me a gobbler! Let's go and put him in with the hen, and I'll settle up with you. Kate, take Laurie indoors and put the kettle on."

"My God," said Laurie in the kitchen. "It really *is* agricultural, isn't it? Well, how are you, Kate? You look blossoming, actually."

"I am," agreed Kate, filling the kettle. "I thought at

first I'd never fit in here, but I'm getting to understand it."

"That's more than I ever would," said Laurie. "I'd hate to leave London. Funny how you've got this hang-up about fitting in, though. I keep telling you, you don't belong anywhere. You're self-contained. A thing on its own. The cat that walks by itself."

"A stray cat," said Kate with a touch of bitterness. "You're not the first person to call me that."

Laurie put his arm around Kate's shoulders and pulled her to him, but, hearing Beth and Alec coming, she detached herself.

"—much hardier," Beth was saying. "The white ones have been overbred, if you ask me. Got time for a cup of coffee, Alec?"

"No, I'd best be off," said Alec. "We're in the middle of haymaking, and Dad's getting a bit restive about me not being there." He nodded in Laurie's direction. "See you again. 'Bye, Kate."

"'Bye, Alec. Thanks a lot for coming."

He gave her a brief grin and his eyes flicked to Laurie as if he was about to make some comment, but he thought better of it and went out.

Laurie fished in his knapsack. "I brought you some garlic," he said. "I know what it is in these country places, you can't get decent garlic anywhere. This is new season's. I had to go to Bertorelli's for it, mind." He brought out three huge garlic bulbs and put them down on the table.

Beth, making coffee, looked at them and said, "That's what you want for your chickens, Kate. Nothing like it for getting rid of worms in poultry. Dogs, too. You ask Alec next time he come."

"Really?" said Kate, interested. "I never knew that."

Laurie closed his eyes as if in pain.

"We haven't quite finished outside," said Beth. "So I'll get on, if you'll excuse me. Kate, will you do some potatoes and make some pastry? There's heaps of rhubarb in the garden."

Lunch was a success, Laurie approving of Beth's braised beef and the fragrant pink rhubarb pie and cream. "No wonder you look so well, Kate," he said.

"It's been nice having someone to cook for," said Beth. "And she's a good little cook herself, too. I'll miss her when she go back."

"I've missed her all the while she's been here," said Laurie sentimentally, but this remark was jumped on at once by Beth, with her ruthless honesty.

"If you'd have taken care of her in the first place, she'd never have come," she said. "Forgive me speaking so plain, but that's the truth."

"The truth as far as you know," agreed Laurie easily. "There's always more to these things than meets the eye." And, adroitly changing the subject, he began to talk about the new design project he was engaged on with Hilary Billinghurst. "My God, that woman's clever," he said. "The things she can do with an airbrush are astonishing. She's got style, too. Long face like a horse, pale blue eyes, high-arched nose—got the snooty look. But then Daddy owns half Dorset, so well she might. But the thing is, with a face like that she still has the cheek to wear her hair in a thirties shingle. Cropped close at the neck, with rows of corrugated iron waves and kiss curls on the cheekbones. Knocks me out."

Kate laughed, but Beth got to her feet disapprovingly and said she must help Peter put the heifers out.

"I don't think she likes me," said Laurie, when Beth had gone out.

"Of course she does," protested Kate. "It's just—Well, you're two very different sorts of people. Did you remember my Rapidograph bit?"

"Of course I did." Laurie delved into the knapsack again. "Here you are. What have you been doing, anyway? Got any work to show me?"

"Yes, heaps," said Kate, glad to be on safer ground. "It's all upstairs in my room. I'll go and get it."

"No need to lug heavy things about." Laurie jumped to his feet. "I'll come and see."

In the bedroom Laurie shut the door, sat down on the bed, and pulled Kate to him. "Katie. Darling Katie. Come on."

Kate returned his kiss, cross with herself rather than with him. Of *course* when he said he would come upstairs he meant that he wanted to make love to her. Why had she not realized it? And why, in all reason, should she now feel a little outraged?

"Someone might come," she said, trying to disengage herself.

"No, they won't," said Laurie. "They've gone to play with their cows and, anyway, Beth's not daft. She knows what I've come for."

"What have you come for?"

"To make you mine, Kate. To love you and kiss you and keep you safe forever."

"You mean—"

"Marry me, Katie. It's all simple now."

"But you said—"

"I know. I felt terrible about Barbara at first. But time does heal. One recovers. How does this smock thing undo? Oh, snaps. Lovely."

"Laurie, I suppose it's being pregnant, but I just don't seem to feel very sexy these days."

"I'm glad," said Laurie, kissing her neck. "With the Hulk lurking about, I wouldn't want you feeling sexy."

"You mean Alec?" Kate laughed. "Oh, Alec's not like that. He honestly is just a friend. He's been ever so kind, but I think of him as a sort of brother. I expect he's got heaps of girl friends at the Young Farmers and that sort of thing."

"He," said Laurie, "is a randy tomcat like any other guy. Darling, aren't you a busty girl now. Beautiful."

"I want to breast feed the baby," said Kate.

Laurie sat up. "Now don't be daft. If you breast

feed it, you've got to take the creature with you wherever you go."

"Yes," agreed Kate placidly, doing up her smock.

"Look, I met a chap from Swiss television the other day who's got a place in Gmunden. He's asked us both to go over there in September. Trips on the lake, bags of wine and food. You'd adore it. But not with a *baby*. Now if it's on the bottle, your mum can have it for a few days, can't she?"

"No, she can't!" said Kate hotly. "In the first place she may be working and in the second place she won't *want* to look after a baby and in the third place I'm not going to part with him to Mum or anyone else, so there!"

"Oh, Lord." Laurie sighed. "You *have* gone motherly, haven't you?" He got up and stared moodily out the window. "Nice view." He turned back. "So I suppose you won't come back to London with me?"

"What, *now*?"

"Yes. That's what I'd planned. Beth can send your things on later. Come on, Katie-cat." He took both Kate's hands in his. "I *need* you."

Kate looked at him carefully, as if to be sure what she was giving up. "No," she said. "I'm not coming back, Laurie."

"You want to have the baby here. Oh, well." He shrugged. "I suppose if you feel settled. . . ."

"It's not just that," said Kate steadily. "I'm not coming back to you ever. You don't want the baby, and it wouldn't be fair to bring a child up like that."

"What are you going to do then?"

"I don't know. I wish I did."

Laurie made a helpless gesture. "Why did I bother?" Depressed and preoccupied, he flipped open the sketchbook that lay on the dressing table. "Hey!" he said with sudden interest. "Are these yours?"

"Yes."

He studied the drawings closely. "Where did you get this patterning technique?"

"I didn't get it anywhere. I just do it."

"But it's super. Like patchwork. Everything shoved in where it fits."

"I'm so awful at perspective, you see," Kate explained.

Exasperated, Laurie slid the drawings together and slapped the sketchbook shut. "You've got everything, haven't you!" he said. "Makes me sick." And he went downstairs.

"Laurie's catching an earlier train," said Kate, when Beth came in. "There's one at four twenty. Do you think we could make it?"

"Yes," said Beth, "if that's what you want."

"Sorry to throw a monkeywrench in the works," said Laurie, "but I've got—"

"Turn the van around, Kate," said Beth. "while I wash my hands."

Trying to show no surprise, Kate went out. She had never driven the van before, and obscurely she felt Beth's instruction to be a sign of support. Very cautiously she backed the van around so that it was ready to leave the yard, then moved over for Beth.

"Got your little bag?" Beth asked Laurie.

"Yes," he said through clenched teeth, "thank you."

The drive to the station was a silent one.

The turkey took to her new mate happily, but after a while Kate found no more of the pointed, brown-spotted eggs in the straw.

"The turkey seems to have stopped laying," she told Beth.

"No, she hasn't," said her aunt positively. "She'll have found a place to lay a clutch of eggs to sit on. You won't find them unless you follow her. Watch her when she's been fed."

For several days the turkey managed to slip away while Kate was busy with pens of broody hens and chicks, but one morning when she was carrying the drinkers around to the yard tap she saw the turkey unobtrusively picking her way past the willow tree. Kate followed at a discreet distance, noticing how the bird turned her small head from side to side as if anxious to preserve her privacy. She reached the hedge that bordered the lane and, with a final glance about her, made her way through it and disappeared from view.

Kate crept after her. Very quietly she parted the

tall grasses and peered down into the hedge. The turkey was sitting in a small hollow lined with dry leaves. Curving her long neck to reach under her breast feathers, she was rearranging the eggs she had already laid. With a last comfortable shuffle she settled herself down. One beady eye, totally black, unlike a chicken's brown-ringed one, glanced up at Kate but showed no sign of alarm. The turkey had already entered the mindless, all-accepting trance of broodiness.

Kate went away quietly. It was strange, she thought, how the turkey's whole defense mechanism was concentrated on her choice of a place in which to lay and her caution in approaching it. Once there and committed to her eggs, she was completely passive.

"The turkey's chosen a funny place for her nest," she said. "Under the hedge by the lane. Miles from anywhere."

"She like to think nobody know where she is," Beth explained. "That make her feel safe."

"Yes," said Kate thoughtfully. "I can understand how she feels."

13

Time dragged. Kate felt heavily burdened, and her back ached. The weather was hot and sultry, increasing her tiredness, and, as she had predicted, her swollen body was too big to fit easily into the driver's seat of the Traveller.

There was not much she could do. Peter seemed to be constantly ahead of her, carrying buckets and filling meal bins and advising her to "Take it easy." She longed for the baby to be born and free her from its heavy, uncomfortable presence.

For a while she continued to milk Freda while Beth milked the heavier-yielding Susannah, but soon Freda, who was due to calve in October, needed milking only in the morning and at last her soft udder contained so little that Beth said, "We'll let her go dry now." Kate missed the comfortable rhythm of milking and felt deprived of the opportunity to exercise her newfound skill. Disconsolately leaning on the cow-shed door, she watched Beth milking Susannah, and one morning Beth got up from the milking stool and said, "Come and finish her off then. I'll go and feed the pigs." But Kate found the Ayrshire hard work. She was an older cow than Freda and her udder was pendulous, so that Kate had to lean down a long way to reach her teats. Kate soon felt cramped and uncomfortable. Her hands ached, and the great udder seemed endlessly full. Susannah's calf had been stillborn and she had refused to foster another, so the long job of milking her could not be avoided. It was too much for Kate. When Beth reappeared at the cowshed door, Kate handed her the half-full bucket wordlessly and went into the house.

She envied the rapid simplicity with which her poultry hatched off their young. Tiny ducklings bobbed on the pond, and the geese escorted their gray-and-yellow offspring across the yard with irritating smugness. The turkey, though, remained on her nest. She had stopped coming to the yard for food each day and sat motionless on her thirteen eggs, almost invisible under the dark hedge.

Since Kate could no longer drive, Beth, whose leg was much better, took her into town when necessary for hospital visits, and so Kate had not seen Alec for some time. In the absence of driving lessons, she took it for granted that there was no reason for him to come. But one morning he rang her up.

"I'm going into Hadham for some sheep netting,"

he said. "Do you want to come along for a look around the market?"

"That would be nice," said Kate gratefully. "Things are a bit boring these days."

"I might even stand you a cup of coffee at Geordie's."

"Thrills!" said Kate, feeling in fact more thrilled than she would admit.

In Hadham, she set off for a browse around the market stalls, having arranged to meet Alec in Geordie's at eleven. Beth had asked her to look for autumn-sown onion seed and Winter Density lettuce, making Kate feel that summer was slipping away. She found the seeds and bought Beth an African violet in a pot as a little present.

She paused at a chemist's window devoted to baby care and stared at the array of diapers and potties, pins and powders and oils and syrups, pink-and-blue brushes and soap dishes. Was there anything she had forgotten? A tiny sundress in orange cotton caught her eyes. It would be lovely to buy pretty things like that if her baby was a girl, she thought.

"Hello!" A cheerful voice interrupted her reverie.

"Tessa! How nice to see you! And you're so *slim*! How's the baby?" Fascinated, Kate peered into the carriage where the infant lay fast asleep, a tiny clenched fist pressed against the downy cheek.

"She's fine," said Tessa happily. "Sleeps all night

now. How are you, though? When are you due?"

"Next Friday," said Kate. "Isn't it awful, this waiting? I feel such a lumping great elephant."

"Ghastly," agreed Tessa. "Sophia was five days late, and I kept getting the house all clean and laying in a store of food in case I was whisked off, then having to do it all again. How's Laurie?"

Kate took a deep breath. This time she was going to get it right. "Tessa," she said, "I ought to have told you this before, only there never seemed to be a chance. I'm not married to Laurie."

"Oh." Absurdly, it was Tessa who blushed. "I'm sorry. I supposed I assumed—"

"No, it was my fault."

"Come to think of it," said Tessa, recovering, "I did wonder for a moment when you turned up with that lovely man in the Land-Rover."

"Alec?" Kate laughed. "No, you're on the wrong track there, too. Alec is just a friend. I was living with Laurie before I came here, and I was going to marry him but—it didn't work. Fatherhood just isn't Laurie's scene."

"What a shame," said Tessa. Then she added persistently, "So how long have you known Alec?"

"Just a few months. I'm living on my aunt's farm, you see, and Alec's father supplies her with feedstuffs. And when she had an accident and couldn't drive, they gave me a lift. They're just one of those very nice families."

"M'm," said Tessa, reserving her opinion. "Look, let's go and have a cup of coffee. If we go to Geordie's, we can sit by the window and keep an eye on Sophia."

"I'm meeting Alec at Geordie's, at eleven," said Kate. "What's the time now?"

"Quarter to. Come on. We can have a chat before he comes." Tessa was being very bright and kind, Kate thought.

Over coffee, Tessa suddenly touched Kate's hand and said, "It doesn't matter, you know. What you told me. I mean, it could happen to anyone. Before I married Michael I had another boyfriend, and—well—it might have happened to me. I was just lucky."

"I wasn't unlucky," said Kate fairly. "I wanted the baby."

Tessa smiled. "Good for you," she said. "What are you going to do afterward? I hope you're not going away."

"I don't know," said Kate. "That's what people keep asking, and I just don't know. I feel as if I'm waiting for something to happen."

"Let's hope it'll be something nice," said Tessa. "Look, isn't that your friend?"

Alec stood outside the café, glancing at his watch.

"Isn't he brown!" said Tessa.

"He's been haymaking," said Kate. She tapped on the window, but Alec did not hear. "I'd better go and tell him where we are," she said. "He hates waiting."

Outside, Alec was smiling down at Sophia, who

had wakened and was plucking with bemused concentration at the satin edge of her blanket.

"Hello," he greeted Kate. "Isn't this a nice baby? Should encourage you no end!"

"She's sweet, isn't she!" Kate beamed. "Her name's Sophia Jane Cooney, and her mother is a friend of mine. Come and meet her!" She suddenly felt much happier. It was so lovely to have friends to introduce to each other.

On the way home Alec said, "What are you going to call your baby?"

"I haven't decided," said Kate. "It seems funny to name someone who isn't a person yet."

"You must have thought about it, though."

"Yes, of course I have. Laurie wanted to call her Josephine if the baby is a girl, but I like Ruth. And anyway, it's got nothing to do with him now."

"Hasn't it? How's that then?"

"I told Laurie I wasn't going back. Not ever."

Alec's eyebrows went up, but all he said was, "What if the baby is a boy?"

"I don't know," said Kate. "I feel a bit blank about that. In a way I'm hoping for a girl. It's quite easy for a girl to be brought up by her mother, I think. It seemed OK for Mum and me, anyway."

"It's never easy," said Alec positively. "It's better when people stay together. They shouldn't rush into choosing a wife so hasty. A mad love affair is no way to start married life."

"Isn't it?" Kate was amused by his vehemence.

"No, it's not. It's the most important thing a man ever does, and yet there's chaps I know take more thought about buying a new tractor than they do about the girl they're going to marry."

"But a girl isn't a tractor," objected Kate, laughing. "You can't size her up as good value for money!"

"No, but you can size her up as good value for life," said Alec. "She's the person you're going to live with and depend on. A farmer's in a fair old muddle without a good wife. You need someone sensible in the house to deal with phone calls and supplies coming and look after any sick stock and be there if the vet come. And anyway, she's going to have your children who'll go on after you, and you want those children to be the right sort of people, don't you? Now your dad married the wrong woman, but he was lucky with you. You've got a head on your shoulders although you're pretty. You've taken after him, you see."

"That's not fair," argued Kate. "Mum's very intelligent as well as being beautiful. It's just that she's not very interested in practical things. And anyway, if what you say is right, what's *my* baby going to be like? She might take after her artistic father and be even less practical than Mum!"

"Artists aren't impractical," said Alec. "There's a lot of rubbish talked abcut art. It's just a creative job you do with your mind and your hands, same as farming.

Your chap's not impractical; he's just blasted selfish. And your babe will be a big, healthy, intelligent, good-looking, artistic farmer."

"It'll be a boy then?" asked Kate smiling.

"Of course it will," said Alec.

It was dark when Kate woke. In recent weeks she had suffered from cramps in her legs, which Dr. McTaggart said was due to the pressure of the baby on a nerve. Quite often she had awakened with the sudden, agonizing pain of a seized-up calf muscle and had sat up in bed to stretch and rub her leg until the bunched fibers had relaxed.

But this was different. Confused and half asleep, with her mind still involved in a dream, Kate felt vaguely cross about the discomfort that had wakened her. The dream ran on, and she swam away with it.

The pain came again, a grasping rigidity that jolted her into full consciousness. She found that she was holding her breath like someone underwater, waiting for the engulfing attack to go so that she could breathe again. The pain subsided. Lying in the darkness, Kate felt hot and rather frightened. Groping for the bedside light, she noticed that the windows were pale blue behind their patterned curtains. Dawn was coming then. The switched-on lamp dismissed all hint of daylight with its electric brilliance. The hands of the alarm clock stood at quarter to four. What an unearthly hour to start having a baby, Kate thought.

And what was today, anyway? The baby wasn't due until Friday. She had been to market with Alec today —no, yesterday. This was Thursday morning then.

Had the pain really happened, or was it just a false alarm? There was no sign of it now. How warm and comfortable beds were in the mornings.

Although Kate was almost asleep again, when the next pain came she was ready for it. She remembered what she had been taught at the prenatal classes. Shallow breathing. Pant like a dog. Relax. The easy advice seemed very difficult to apply now, in the face of this gripping contraction. But Kate found that by breathing as she had been told with the upper part of her lungs and leaving the pain to run its course uninterfered with, everything seemed easier. It was almost as if she had divided herself into two halves, leaving her lower half to attend to its own affairs. When the contraction slacked, she looked at the clock. Five past four.

Kate decided that she had better wake Beth. If she waited too long, they would be going to hospital in the busy part of the early morning, interrupting Beth's routine of milking and feeding. She got up, put on her dressing gown and slippers, and went along to her aunt's room. She tapped on the door but got no reply, so she opened it and went in, soundless on the thick carpet. The light from the corridor shone across Beth's face as she lay asleep. With her gray hair released from its customary tie and spread in disarray across the pillow, she looked unfamiliar. "Beth," whispered Kate. "Beth, please wake up."

Beth was awake at once. "Have you started?" she asked.

"Yes," said Kate.

"Go back to bed, my lovey, and I'll be with you in a minute," said Beth. In an amazingly short time she appeared in Kate's room, fully dressed and with her hair tied back into its normal ponytail. "Have you been awake long?" she asked.

"About half an hour. I had another pain just now—that's the third—and I thought before you start milking and everything—"

Beth laughed. "Don't you worry about that, my dear. There's always Peter. But I think we'd best get you into hospital just the same. I'll ring for an ambulance and make a cup of tea."

"It seems silly to call the ambulance out," said Kate, feeling oddly embarrassed. "I mean, I'm not *ill.* Couldn't we go in the van?"

"No, we couldn't," said Beth firmly. "Bumping about on that hard seat is the last thing you want." And she went out.

Kate began to get dressed, but she was interrupted by another contraction. She sat down on the bed, then, finding it difficult to relax in a sitting position, lay down. Perhaps Beth was right about the van, she thought.

It was gray daylight when the ambulance came. A

cheerful red-haired ambulance man came in. "Going to be a nice day," he said. "Always a good sign when it's misty first thing. How are you, my love?"

"All right," said Kate.

"Waters broken yet?"

"No."

"Feeling sick at all?"

"No."

"And how often are your contractions?"

"About ten minutes."

"That's fine," he said. "We'd best be getting along then."

"I'll come in my van," said Beth. "Then I can get back."

In the ambulance, Kate looked up through the tinted windows and saw the tops of trees wheeling by. Despite the soft red blanket that covered her, her hands and feet felt cold.

"All right are you, love?" asked the ambulance man.

"Yes, thank you," said Kate. She had not had a contraction since she left the house and was beginning to feel that this journey was a mistake.

At the hospital, Kate said good-bye to the nice ambulance man, who handed her into the care of a West Indian nurse.

"Come along, please," said the nurse. Kate looked around anxiously and saw to her relief that Beth was just coming in, holding Kate's suitcase. The nurse led them to a lift, then along a corridor, and through double doors to the maternity ward, where she ushered them into a small room with a few chairs and a desk in it.

"Sit down, please," she said. "I'll get Staff Nurse." She bustled out again. "New admission!" they heard her call. "Anyone seen Staff?"

After a while a more senior nurse came in. "Sorry to keep you," she said. "Things have been a bit hectic. You are Mrs.—?"

"Carling," said Kate.

There was the inevitable form to fill in. Then the nurse said, "I'll show you your bed in Prenatal, Mrs. Carling, and there'll be a few more things to do. Come along."

Following the nurse with Beth, Kate felt glad after all that she had come in before her labor was any further advanced. All this walking about must be dreadful for anyone whose contractions were coming thick and fast, she thought.

"Now," said the nurse, flicking the curtains around the bed, "pop into your night things, and someone will be along to give you your bath and enema. And I expect your friend will want to be getting home."

Beth looked impassive as usual, but when the nurse had gone, she said, "I know these modern hospitals have got marvelous equipment, but there's a lot to be said for having babies at home. Still, I'd best be off."

"All right," said Kate, trying not to feel abandoned. "Thanks for everything."

Unexpectedly, Beth kissed Kate and held her in a motherly hug. "Don't you worry," she said. "You'll have a lovely baby, and things are going to be all right. You'll see."

Kate nodded wordlessly. A very young nurse with short fair hair put her head in through the curtains and said, "Mrs. Carling? Do you want any help undressing? I've come to give you your bath." She seemed no older than Kate herself and looked so pop-eyed and tentative that Kate laughed. "Come in," she said.

"I'll be off then," said Beth again. This time she just gave Kate a comforting nod, but she turned as she parted the curtains. "Whatever you do," she said, "don't worry about those chickens." And then she went.

The little nurse giggled. "You hear some funny parting words in here," she said, "but that takes the cake."

14

Back in bed after the discomfort of routine preparation, Kate felt depressed. She had still not had a contraction since leaving Willow Farm. Clearly it was all a false alarm.

"Never mind," the little nurse said. "It happens to lots of people, especially with first babies. Sometimes it's a week or more before they really get going."

"Thanks a lot," said Kate. She stared gloomily around the long ward with its high, chapellike windows. The woman in the bed opposite looked up from her pink knitting. "You in labor?" she asked.

"I thought I was," said Kate. "I was having contractions every ten minutes, but as soon as I got here it all stopped."

"You'll soon be off again," the woman said comfortably. "I've been here three weeks, and I'm not due for another ten days. Blood pressure."

"Three weeks! That's awful!" said Kate.

Conversation lapsed, and Kate, warm now, began

to feel very sleepy after her predawn start to the day.

"Dinner, dear!" The loud announcement awoke Kate with a start. She rolled over to look up at the speaker and was at once seized by a pain so welcome but so agonizing that Kate made a noise somewhere between a laugh and a sob.

"Fish pie," said the green uniformed helper implacably, putting a tray on Kate's bed table. To her surprise, Kate was quite hungry, but the fish pie and subsequent apricot crumble were three times interrupted by violent contractions, and she soon gave up the effort to eat any more. When the helper had cleared away the dishes, Kate lay down and gave her full attention to what was happening to her. Although she was glad that it had not turned out to be a false alarm, the severity of the pain frightened her. Surely if the prenatal advice was right, she ought not to feel so bad! She turned uneasily in the bed, rubbing her hand across her hot face.

"On your way, are you?" the pink-knitting woman inquired. Panting, Kate nodded.

"Keep an eye on Mrs. Carling, nurse!" shouted the pink knitter, who had clearly achieved a senior status in the ward. "She's going to have that baby any minute!"

The head nurse, sleeves rolled up, whisked the curtains around Kate's bed and turned the bedclothes back. "Knees up, my pet," she instructed. "Just relax while I have a look-see. Good girl! Yes, we'll take you down to Delivery. Nurse!" She disappeared through the curtains and sometime later a stretcher was wheeled alongside Kate's bed.

"Roll over, Mrs. Carling, dear. That's it."

Kate found it amazingly difficult to move. She seemed to be literally in the grip of a force far stronger than herself. The accelerating severity and frequency of the contractions were becoming almost more than she could bear, and it took all her self-control to prevent the pain from engulfing her mind as well as her body. After the journey on the stretcher, Kate had to make another deeply unwelcome effort to roll herself onto the bed in the delivery room. The contractions were almost continuous now, with none of the pain-free spaces that had allowed her to recover a little. Everything seemed to hurt, even the things she could see. Shiny metal pipes ran along the wall, and her eyes followed them until cut off by the metal table near her bed. Again and again her vision ran along the pipes to the table and back to the pipes until it began to seem that the hard metal edges were a cage enclosing the small tortured animal that was herself. Panting helplessly, she began to sob. It was too much. She was drowning in pain.

People were around her, talking. Moving things about.

"Just a little injection, Kate." It was a man's voice,

vaguely familiar. Kate felt the needle's stab in her thigh with a different awareness.

"Here, pet, hold this." A mask was put into Kate's hand. Gas and air analgesia, a part of her mind recognized. "Breathe in, pet. It doesn't smell. Pant into the mask. That's right." Kate began to feel weightless and mercifully remote. The pain was still there, but it wasn't so close. She didn't need to sob anymore. The pipes had gone. There was darkness. Or was it light. Everything was happening faster, like being on a fairground ride gone crazy. There was a sudden, bursting warm flood. "Aah!" It was Kate's own voice. "Nurse! I—"

"There's a good girl," said a cheerful voice, close to her. "That's the waters broken. You *are* getting on well."

Quick, skillful hands lifted and rearranged her. There was a dry sheet, warm, comfortable. The contractions had stopped. Kate let the mask fall away from her face and breathed in the open air, grateful for the remission.

A new, completely different pain grasped her. This was a strong, downward cramp of muscle clearly understandable as the mechanics of childbirth. Instead of needing to keep her awareness outside it, Kate was glad to be involved. Time passed, and, as before, the contractions increased in severity. She gasped deeply into the mask, straining with each contraction, astonished by the power of this force that possessed her, pushing and pushing. . . . Where had all the people gone? Would this baby never be born? She gave a little cry of despair.

"You're doing fine, pet." The people *were* there.

"Push now, Kate. That's it." The man's voice.

"Good girl. Another little push. Good . . . good."

Somebody wiped her face. Somebody was holding her knee up as she lay on her side. Suddenly the pain was immense. Overwhelming.

"Don't push now, Kate." The man sounded urgent. "Pant for a minute. Try not to push."

Kate's whole body was desperately demanding to push down. Panting shallowly, she tried to stop it as the voice had asked but a huge solidness was welling up, forcing its way out. "I can't!" she heard herself gasp.

"One little push, pet."

"Aaah!" The push was immense, the triumph of its success devastating. Warm and hard against her leg, Kate felt the baby's head blossom out, and then the slippery body.

"Five thirty-two," said somebody. "Male." There was activity going on, but it was at some distance from Kate. There was no pain. She could move again. She heard a spluttering cry.

"You've got a little boy, Kate," said the familiar voice.

"Doctor Marsh!" said Kate. "Have you been here all the time?"

He smiled at her. "All the time," he said.

A nurse brought the baby, wrapped in a soft white blanket, and carefully put him in Kate's arms. "Mind his head now. Keep your hand under it."

"Oh," breathed Kate. The baby had stopped crying and was nuzzling at his fist. He had dark, silky hair all over his head, and, far from being red and crumpled as people always said newborn babies were, his face was smooth and downy. For a moment his eyes opened with unseeing perplexity, and then they shut again and he resumed his dabbing exploration of his fist.

"That child's hungry," said the nurse, standing with her gloved hands on her hips triumphantly.

"Can I feed him?" asked Kate eagerly.

"You won't have any milk until tomorrow, pet, but you can put him to the breast by all means. It helps the womb to contract, anyway."

Kate had never known such pure happiness in her life before. She was warm and alive, and the sudden ceasing of pain created an opposite state of physical bliss. The dazzling surgical lights were like pure sunshine, the white sterile gowns angelic, and the baby himself so amazingly precious that Kate could hardly bear to hand him back to the nurse after his short suckle.

"Mustn't make yourself sore, pet, or you'll have difficulty feeding him when your milk comes," the nurse explained, tucking the baby into his crib.

"What does he weigh?" asked Kate. And then, "Oh!"

"Another contraction? That's the afterbirth," said the nurse. "Just pant into your gas and air for a minute, pet. That's it."

"Eight pounds four," Dr. Marsh told Kate, beaming all over his plump face. "A whopper! That's why I didn't want you to push too hard at the moment of crowning, Kate, but you did splendidly. Just a couple of stitches, that's all. It won't hurt."

Kate didn't mind about the stitches. She didn't mind about anything. A nurse washed her hands and face for her, and the warmth of the water and softness of the towel were wonderful. Everything was wonderful.

15

Kate was moved to the maternity ward in time for supper. The baby in his crib was wheeled along too and put at the foot of her bed. She still felt very happy and peaceful, and yet there was an odd sense of loss, too. She had been used to the heavy, restless presence of the baby inside her, and now that it was gone she felt empty and alone.

The other women in the ward welcomed the new arrival with cries of "What did you have, dear?" and "What does he weigh?"

Kate answered them with a touch of pride. "Eight pounds four."

"Gosh, what a size!" they said. Then, inevitably, they asked, "Is your husband tall?"

"Not very," Kate said. And to escape further conversation, she pulled the bedclothes up to her chin and pretended to be sleepy, although her mind was briskly active. She already wished that she could leave hospital, detesting the enforced company of these other women with their inquisitive eyes and endless gossip.

Beth came in the evening, with Peter. She seemed to be walking stiffly, Kate thought, but Beth was so delighted with the baby that nothing else mattered.

"They won't mind if I pick him up, will they?" she said, lifting the baby out of his crib. "He's awake anyway, aren't you, my pet?" Her ugly face glowed with delight, and Peter, too, smiled with unaccustomed tenderness as he leaned forward to look at the child.

"I'm glad you came, Peter," said Kate, touched that he should have shown so much interest. "I thought you'd be busy combining."

"Thought I'd best keep an eye on her," said Peter, nodding at Beth with a return to his usual taciturnity. "She's hurt her knee again. Winter barley's all in, anyway."

"You haven't had another accident, have you?" Kate asked Beth anxiously. "You seemed all right this morning." Was it really only this morning that she had come here? It seemed a world ago.

"I turned on it a bit awkward or something," said Beth. "It's only an excuse for Peter to come. He wanted to see the baby as much as I did. What are you going to call him, Kate?"

Kate had made up her mind. "Thomas Rowley," she said firmly. "Thomas is such a nice round, simple name. I thought of it that first morning when Tom and Alec

Fairchild came. You don't think he'll mind, do you?"

"Most people would take it as a compliment," said Peter, "having a child named after them. I reckon Tom will."

"And Rowley after my father," Kate went on. "It's a nice name to keep in the family, and since Dad's gone away, there's not likely to be two Rowley Carlings about."

"You never know," said Beth. Then, changing the subject, she added, "Did you see I'm wearing the blouse you made? That's a lovely fit."

"So you are!" Kate beamed. "I've never seen it on you before."

"I was keeping it for a special occasion," said Beth. "And you couldn't ask for anything more special than this. I rang your mother up, by the way. She sends her love and says she hope to come and see you tomorrow."

"That'll be nice," said Kate. She wanted to ask whether Alec knew, but somehow she hesitated. Remembering how the nurse had taken him for Kate's husband when they had visited Beth, she could understand that he wouldn't want to come to the maternity ward. So there was no point in asking.

"Has my turkey hatched off yet?" she inquired.

"I never thought to look," said Beth. "When did she set?"

"I'm not sure," said Kate. "She went sort of gradually."

"I'll have a look tomorrow," Beth promised.

Kate felt imprisoned. "I wish I could come home," she said. "I miss all the birds and things."

Peter smiled. "They'll wait for you," he said.

And with that, Kate had to be content.

Nancy came the next day at afternoon visiting time. She wore a floating chiffon dress with a trailing scarf of the same stuff and carried an extravagant bouquet of red roses. Nigel, as always, stood a little behind her.

"Darling!" She kissed Kate. "Roses for you. What a clever girl you are! I can't get over being a granny."

"Super baby," said Nigel, hands in pockets and head on one side as he gazed down at the crib.

"Isn't he *lovely*!" agreed Kate.

Nancy Carling sat down and gave the baby her full attention. "He really is a beautiful child," she pronounced. "And you're all right, darling? It wasn't too frightful?"

"It was marvelous," said Kate. "I mean, it did hurt like anything, but I felt I was *doing* something. I'd love to have another one."

"Steady," said Nigel.

Nancy laughed, and then stopped laughing. "Darling," she said, "there's something I'd better tell you before anyone else does. It's about Laurie. I think he's living with another woman."

"Hilary Billinghurst?" asked Kate.

"I don't know *who*," said her mother, shocked. "But

when Beth rang to say you'd had the baby, I was setting out for my evening class at the Central and I didn't have a chance to ring Laurie until afterward. Actually, it was quite a long time afterward, because Nigel and I had a drink to celebrate."

Nigel put his hand to his head and closed his eyes.

"So it was nearly midnight when I rang," Nancy continued. "And this girl answered. 'It's for you, darling,' she said. And I'm sure they were in bed, Kate. Telephones make such a *gropy* noise when they're passed from hand to hand in bed."

"There is a phone by the bed," Kate remembered. "What did he say?"

"He sounded terribly restrained. Kept saying, 'Thank you very much' and 'I'll ring you tomorrow.' I think he was pretending I was an agent ringing about a job or something."

Kate laughed. "Poor Laurie! How awful to be rung up when you're in bed with someone and told you're a father!"

"Embarrassing," agreed Nigel.

"So you don't mind?" Nancy asked.

Kate gave a little sigh. "I *can't* mind, Mum. Laurie came to ask me to go back with him—I told you in my letter—and I wouldn't. It wasn't right, Mum. I'm sorry. I'm sorry about the baby if he's going to make things awkward, but he's so lovely. . . ." Suddenly she was almost in tears.

Her mother responded at once. "Oh, come on, my

chickie, don't cry." She hugged her. "He's a *beautiful* baby, and you were quite right to have him. Don't you worry about a thing. There's plenty of time to decide what you're going to do."

There was the awful question again. What was she going to do? The baby was born now. She couldn't put off making a decision forever.

"When are you two getting married?" she asked, putting it off a little longer. "You seem to be taking your time about it."

Nancy and Nigel exchanged glances.

"Actually," said Nancy, "we decided not to. I suppose it sounds a bit mad, but we both thought—well, *why*? We're independent people with lives of our own, but living together gives us all the benefits of marriage and none of the snags."

"Nice work if you can get it," said Nigel. He grinned at Nancy affectionately and added, "And I've got it!"

"That'll do, Nigel," said Nancy primly. She turned back to Kate. "Where can I get a vase?" she inquired. "These roses must go into water."

"Ask the girl in an orange smock," said Kate. "She'll get you one from the utility room." It was a relief to be asked a question she could answer.

That evening Beth came again, bringing an untidily wrapped parcel, which turned out to be from Annie at the Silver Snack Bar. It contained a loudly striped crib blanket knitted on huge needles in pink and blue.

"Do for boy or girl. See I'm not daft mate," her note said.

Kate laughed but was secretly touched. "Dear Annie," she said. "I must look her up when I go back to London."

There was a note from Alec, too, written on an invoice form with the printed heading, "Thos. Fairchild and Son, Millers Etc." It said, "Delighted to welcome the Young Farmer. Busy with harvest just now, hope to see you soon. Mum and Dad send congratulations too. Love, Alec."

"How did he know?" asked Kate.

"I rang them up, of course," said Beth. "Mrs. Fairchild was delighted. Wanted to know all about it and sends her love."

"How nice of her," said Kate.

There was a pause. Then Beth said, "I'm worried about old Glyn. He seem a bit under the weather."

"Is he?" Kate was concerned. "Have you had the vet?"

"Not yet. He'll be up this week to dehorn some calves. I'll get him to take a look at Glyn if he's not better."

"It won't be anything serious," said Kate. "He's always been so fit."

"Yes," agreed Beth, "he's a grand old dog."

At afternoon visiting time the next day Tessa came, delighted to be back in the ward and reveling in the nurses' inquiries after Sophia Jane. She brought a box of chocolates and several magazines and was ecstatic over Thomas Rowley. She and Kate thoroughly enjoyed exchanging details of birth weights, feeding habits, and the odd foibles of the other women in the ward, and then Tessa asked, "How's Alec?"

"All right, I expect," said Kate.

"Hasn't he been to see you?"

"Well, it's harvest time," said Kate.

"H'm." Tessa pursed her lips thoughtfully and then was struck by an idea. "Tell you what. Come and have a meal with us one night, you and Alec. When are you leaving hospital?"

"Sunday," said Kate. "But I don't know if—"

"Let's say Tuesday," pursued Tessa. "All right?"

"I'll have to let you know," said Kate. "I can't answer for Alec."

"Of course you can't. I'll ring you on Monday night." Tessa got out her diary. "Now what's your number? And mind. I'm not taking no for an answer!"

Kate laughed. "You may have to," she said.

Kate felt remarkably well. In a few days she was tidying her own bed and carrying bowls of washing water to the more recent arrivals in the ward. The measured routine of hospital life became increasingly irksome, and she longed to be back at Willow Farm.

"Don't rush about too much," the floor nurse cautioned her. "Your uterus is still shrinking back to its normal size, and it'll take a long time if you don't rest enough. Now go and lie down for a while."

Reluctantly Kate obeyed and, being much more tired than she had realized, fell fast asleep. That night, having slept too long in the afternoon, she lay awake in the dim-lit ward, irritated by the sleeping noises of the other women and plagued by the unhappy problem of what to do when she left hospital. If only she had done better at school, she thought miserably, she would have more chance of finding a decent job to support herself and the baby. As it was, what could she do? She had no skills of any sort. As Laurie had rightly said, she was totally irresponsible. She should never have had little Thomas Rowley. Her beautiful, beloved baby was a dreadful mistake. Hot and wretched, she began to cry.

"Kate." The night nurse switched Kate's bed light on. "What's the matter, sweetie?"

Kate buried her face in her pillow, unable to stop crying and fearing that the other women would hear her.

The nurse sat on the edge of her bed and reached across for a Kleenex from the box on Kate's night stand. "Listen," she whispered, when Kate had recovered a little. "Pop your dressing gown on, and come in the duty room. It's miserable lying there in the dark."

Things seemed less awful in the brightly lit duty room.

"I was just going to make some cocoa," said the nurse, whose name, Kate saw from her badge, was Ms. Martin. "You'd like some, wouldn't you?"

"Yes, please," said Kate listlessly. It was difficult to stop crying. Tears just welled up endlessly.

"Lots of people get this fearful depression when they've had a baby," said Ms. Martin. "It's all right for the first few days, then bang. Utter despair."

"What have they got to despair about?" said Kate. "They've got husbands. They belong somewhere."

Ms. Martin shook her head as she poured hot milk into two mugs. "If only you knew," she said. "Being married doesn't solve all problems. I've had married women sitting here whose lives are in such a muddle that they'd envy you."

"*Me*?" said Kate. "Why?"

"Well, look at you! You're young and pretty and intelligent, and you've got your whole life before you. You're free to do whatever you like."

"Whatever I can," corrected Kate.

Ms. Martin shrugged. "Put it that way if you like. But it's your choice, isn't it?"

"That's the trouble!" said Kate, tormented. "I keep asking, what shall I do? And I don't *know*. The more I think about it the worse it gets."

"Ah. Now that's where you're making a mistake," said the nurse. "You're trying to make a decision before a choice has offered itself. Don't try to force things along. You don't have to. Just let it be, as the

Beatles said. Calm down. Let your mind settle. It's like muddy water at the moment, all shaken up. When it settles, you'll know what you want."

"Will I?" said Kate dubiously.

"Yes, you will." Ms. Martin sounded quite positive. "Just do whatever you have to, and you'll find yourself presented with alternatives. All you have to say is yes or no."

"I can't believe that."

"It's true. Now when are you going home?"

"Sunday."

"So you've got another three days here. Use them to get all the rest you can. Don't do so much pottering about that you fall asleep in the afternoon. The trick is to try and just *be,* the way animals are. Have you ever seen a cow with her calf?"

"Oh, yes!" said Kate, brightening up. "Lots! I live on a farm, you see, with my aunt. At least, I have for the last few months."

Ms. Martin eyed her shrewdly. "You don't want to leave it, do you?"

Kate hesitated. What was the truth? All she had to do was say yes or no.

"No," she said.

Why hadn't she realized it before? Half her misery sprang from the thought that she would have to leave Willow Farm. And she didn't want to.

Ms. Martin, with her cocoa mug clasped in her pink, scrubbed hands, nodded slowly. "That's a start," she said. "If it turns out that you do have to leave, perhaps you can find a job on another farm. Now, have you finished your cocoa?"

"Yes, thank you."

"Then off you go back to bed. I'll come and tuck you in in a minute."

But when Ms. Martin came down the ward, Kate was fast asleep.

Beth had come every day at evening visiting time, sometimes with Peter and sometimes alone. Tonight she came alone, walking stiffly down the ward with the slight limp that seemed to have become permanent. She carried a bunch of asters.

"Getting toward autumn," she said, laying the pink and purple flowers on Kate's locker. "How are you today?"

"I'm fine," said Kate. "How are *you*? You still seem to be limping."

"Seem I've got a bit of arthritis in it," said Beth. "Blasted thing."

There was a pause. Kate's mind was full of last night's conversation with Ms. Martin. It was amazing that a complete stranger should have said so much in so few words.

"Beth," she said, "I want to ask you something."

"Go on."

"When I came to Willow Farm, it was because I

was having the baby. I thought—well, everyone thought—when I'd had it I'd go back to London."

Beth waited patiently.

"Mum's been helping with my keep, which is sweet of her, and I can't expect her to go on doing it. What I was thinking was, if I got a job in Hadham, could I stay on at the farm for a bit? I just don't want to go back to London." Kate blundered on, not waiting for an answer. "Only I know you like to be alone really, and I'd quite understand if you felt you'd had enough."

"I've been thinking about that," said Beth. "When your mother first rang up, I wondered what I'd let myself in for. Like you say, I'm not much of a one for company. But I've got fond of you, my dear, and you can stay as long as you want. There's just one thing, though."

"What?"

"This blasted arthritis. Dr. McTaggart says it will get worse rather than better. That mean, sooner or later I'll have to give up the farm."

Kate nodded. It was a truth that had to be faced. Alec had talked about it in the Land-Rover on that very first day. "What will you do?" she asked.

Beth looked a little embarrassed. "This may come as a bit of a surprise from an old thing like me, but I'm thinking of getting married again."

"To Peter?"

"Oh. So you know about that, do you?"

"I should think everybody knows," said Kate, smiling. "You can see by the way he looks at you. He adores you."

Beth turned rather pink. "He's wanted to marry me for years but—I don't know. Everyone thought I'd sell the farm when Jack died, but I didn't want to give it up. And I couldn't turn to someone else, not straight from Jack. Peter knew that."

Kate nodded. "Yes, he would."

"Anyway, if we get married, Peter's cottage would be big enough for us. I'd have a nice big greenhouse and keep some poultry. Give up the cattle."

"And sell the farm?"

"Sell the house and small buildings, and the home paddock with it. Make a nice place for children to keep ponies or something. We'd keep the land—for a few years, anyway, while Peter can work it—and we'd want the barn and granary and tractor sheds. Tom's always said he'd like the farm, but I don't see that he'd need the house."

Kate tried to look calm and interested, fighting down misery. No sooner had she discovered her true desire than it was snatched away. Now the old questions were laid bare again, raw as wounds.

"I've never quite understood how Peter fits in," she said, thrusting the unhappy thoughts away. "Is his cottage tied to the farm?"

"It was," said Beth. "He came to us years ago as

head cowman. Then Jack offered him the purchase of the cottage. Peter's father was a timber merchant, you see. Did very well. He left Peter quite a lot of money, and when Jack died, I sold him those fields the other side of the lane. It helped with the death duties. So Peter's really got his own little farm over there, and he shares the profits on this one for doing the arable work."

"I see," said Kate. "Well, I think it's a lovely idea for you to get married. You know each other so well, it seems the natural thing to do. Will you put the house up for sale straight away?"

"Good gracious, no," said Beth. She looked at Kate with concern. "I've upset you, haven't I?"

"Of course not," Kate lied stoutly, but tears welled up and she bent her head to hide them, cursing herself for being so silly. "Ever since I had the baby," she managed to say, "I've gotten all emotional."

"Of course you have," said Beth. "You always feel like that when you've had a babe." She put her warm, rough hand over Kate's. "Now don't you worry. I shan't do anything for a long while yet. I just thought you'd better know how things are, that's all. It seem more fair."

Kate nodded.

"Day after tomorrow," Beth continued, "you come home. And I'm really looking forward to it. That'll be lovely, having a babe in the house again. Oh, and your turkey's hatched off."

"Has she?" Kate looked up eagerly. "How many's she got?"

"Ten. That's not bad out of thirteen eggs. I took a coop around to where she hatched, and Peter pegged out a wire netting run for her. Young turkeys do better away from chickens."

"Isn't that lovely! I can't wait to see them," said Kate. Then she added, "Oh, how's Glyn, by the way?"

Beth looked down at her hands. "I had him put down yesterday," she said. "Vet said he had cancer. 'Feel here,' he said. 'It's bigger than a golf ball.' That's why he hadn't been eating, of course. It was blocking the entrance to his stomach. So Mr. Main injected him straight away, just where he lay in front of the Aga. He never knew."

"Oh, Beth, I am sorry," said Kate wretchedly. "You'll miss him so much."

"That come to all of us," said Beth. She got to her feet stiffly. "I only hope I go as easy as he did. 'Bye-'bye, Kate. See you again tomorrow."

Kate wept when Beth had gone, but this time her tears were not for herself.

16

Kate was feeding little Thomas Rowley—she still could not decide which name to use—when the nurse brought the mail around next morning. "One for you, dear," she said, dropping a letter on Kate's night stand. Craning her neck, Kate saw that the letter was from Laurie.

Replete, the baby stopped sucking and went to sleep. Cradling his head carefully, Kate put him against her shoulder and rubbed his back gently to bring up his wind. He duly burped and continued to sleep. Kate reached for Laurie's letter.

Dear Kate,
So my little Josephine is not to be. I should have anticipated a disappointment, I suppose, since the fates have run so firmly against us. I wish you and your son all good fortune.
It will, I know, sound utterly squalid, but I must remind you of the money I lent you last spring. It is of course obvious that you did not use it for its intended

purpose. I am at present between jobs and—to put it crudely—broke. So if you could possibly repay the loan, I would be grateful.

For business reasons, Hilary has moved in with me. We work very well together, and she has a lot of valuable contacts. I thought you might be interested to see the proofs of our first project—a series of wall posters designed to cover a hoarding-sized space. The buyer gets these numbered sheets and sticks them up himself. Your primitive style influenced me to some extent—I'm sure you will be flattered.

Write to me sometimes. I will want to know how our joint creation progresses. Thinking of what we were to each other, the old-fashioned term for him is right. He is truly a love-child.

Good-bye, Katie-cat.

With affection and regret,

Laurie.

Kate picked up the enclosed sheet of paper and unfolded it. She laughed and then felt angry. The designs were lifted straight from her own paintings of Willow Farm, with figures, trees, hills, and buildings fitted in whichever way up happened to slot into the pattern. They were more sophisticated than Kate's work, drawn with a professional slickness that she could never achieve, but their derivation was obvious. Kate's annoyance gave way to an optimistic idea. If Laurie thought her paintings worth imitating, perhaps other people might like them too. Beth's son David had said they were saleable. But even if she sold lots of them, they would never make enough money to pay for the Traveller. Kate sighed. It would have to go. She had always known she would probably have to sell it, but it would have been nice to have taken her test first. And how could she get a job in Hadham without transport?

With the baby in the crook of her arm, Kate got out of bed and went down the ward to get clean diapers for him. There was no point in worrying. There was nothing she could do about it as yet.

When Beth came that afternoon she had a strange man with her, a tall, sunburned figure with graying hair whom Kate did not instantly recognize. Then he held his arms out and said with a grin she knew at once, "Well, how's my little girl?"

"Dad!" gasped Kate. And there was such laughing and hugging that it was a long time before anyone said anything else. Then Beth explained, "I was just leaving to come here, and he drove into the yard."

"Hired a car at the airport, and here I am," said Kate's father with an Australian twang that was strange to her. "Let's have a look at my grandson." He scooped the baby out of his crib and held him up, tiny in the brawny arms with their rolled-up sleeves. "My, he's a beauty!" He beamed at the baby, then sat down on Kate's bed, still cradling Thomas Rowley. He looked at his daughter and shook his head. "What

I've missed!" he said. Then he laughed again, bursting with delight and pride and sheer happiness. "It's marvelous to see you!"

"Have you come back for good?" asked Kate.

"No, just a couple of weeks. Beth here rang me up and told me the news, and I just came."

"You rang *Australia*? Beth!"

"Well," said Beth defensively, "he had a right to know he'd got a grandson." But she could not repress a triumphant grin. "Anyway," she added, "it's time old hurts were forgotten. You two have been separated quite long enough."

"You can say that again," agreed Kate's father. He shook his head. "To think of all those wasted years. Things might have turned out a bit different if I'd been around. Still"—he swept away all gloomy thoughts—"who'd want to change anything? I've got a great little family out in Australia and a beautiful daughter here—not to mention a marvelous grandson! Now, Kate, when are you getting out of here?"

"Tomorrow," said Kate.

"Well, heck, today's as good as tomorrow. You can come with us now, can't she, Beth?"

"Oh, I can't!" Kate, conditioned by hospital discipline, was scandalized. "You can't go out until you've seen the doctor and been discharged. And he won't be around until tomorrow."

"Rubbish!" Her father jumped to his feet, still holding the baby, and strode off down the ward in pursuit of a nurse. "Hey, nurse! Here a minute!" But he came back cross and frustrated. "She says it's not up to her. Who *is* it up to then?"

"I'll have a word with the head nurse," said Beth. She limped away toward the duty room. Kate and her father watched her go.

"I'm sorry to see her like that," said Kate's father. "She always had such energy. A bomb of a girl."

"It's a shame," agreed Kate. "She's thinking of selling the farm, you know. She's going to marry Peter."

"After all these years! Good old Peter."

"It's been marvelous, living with Beth. It was awful at first, and I thought I'd never fit in but—" Kate found herself pouring out all that had happened to her and all her worries and uncertainties as easily as if she had last seen her father yesterday.

Beth came back smiling. "I had a word with Dr. McTaggart on the phone, and he said that's all right," she said. "You can go home right away."

"But I haven't any clothes!" said Kate.

"When your dad turned up," said Beth, "I nipped in and packed your bag, just in case. It's in the car."

"So *that's* what you were up to!" said Kate's father. He thrust the baby into Kate's arms. "I'll go and get it."

"Oh, Beth," said Kate, "you are marvelous!"

" 'Course I'm not," said Beth. "You just need a bit of common sense, that's all."

Kate's outdoor clothes felt strange. Willow Farm,

too, seemed faintly unfamiliar. The kitchen lacked the presence of Glyn on the hearthrug in front of the Aga, and outside, although the sun was warm and the leaves were still green on the trees, there was a smell of harvest and the light wind held a new freshness. "It's autumn," said Kate. She went from place to place happily renewing acquaintances. "Haven't the ducklings grown!" she said. Then, coming to the pen by the hedge, she added, "Oh, and look at the little turkeys! Aren't they gorgeous!"

Small heads, each with a tiny knob above the beak, popped out from under the turkey's wings as she brooded her family.

"I never thought she'd do as well as that," said Kate. "She made such a scruffy old nest. It didn't look as if she meant business at all."

"But she did," said her father. He put his arm around Kate and added, "You're just as bad yourself, turning up here with no more than a few feathers, and now look at you—settled down with a family!"

"Hardly settled down," said Kate, her face clouding.

"Come on in the house," said Beth firmly. "It's time for tea."

The baby woke Kate early the next morning, crying for his feeding. She lifted him out of his crib and pulled the curtains back from the window. Outside the mist lay heavy over the fields. It was going to be another warm day.

In the kitchen later, Beth said, "There's an old boiler in the shed, all nice and clean. Jane used to dump her baby's used diapers in it, in cold water, and boil them up each morning."

A routine, Kate realized, was being established. It was rather comforting. Her father came across the yard in a pair of Peter's Wellingtons that were wet with dew. "How's my girl this morning?" he asked, giving her a kiss.

"I'm fine," said Kate. "I thought you were still in bed. I was just going to bring you a cup of tea."

"At eight o'clock?" said her father. "Good Lord, no. I've been up since half past six—habit, I suppose. Harvest looks good, Beth. What have you got out there on the ten-acre field? Porthos, is it?"

"Ark Royal," said Beth, "but I might go back to Proctor next year." A long discussion on barley varieties developed while Kate busied herself frying bacon.

"Do you keep livestock?" she asked her father, when the conversation lapsed.

"Oh, Lord, yes. Two thousand head of sheep and a big herd of cattle. Murray Greys—marvelous breed, that. Do you have them here?" And they were off again.

Over breakfast Kate said, "I can't imagine what your farm is like. Huge, I suppose, and very mechanized."

"Has to be," said her father. "We don't have these farms like little gardens that you've got in England, you know." He reached for the butter. "Kate," he said, "why don't you come back with me? You and the baby would fit in fine out there. You know I married again?"

Kate nodded. "Beth told me."

"There's three young brothers of yours would love to meet you," her father went on. "And Mary's a great girl. There's a home and a family ready waiting for you. Now why don't you?"

"Heavens," said Kate. "Do I have to decide now?"

Her father laughed. "Of course not," he said. 'I'm not going back for a fortnight."

A car scrunched to a stop in the yard. A door banged, and Alec Fairchild walked into the kitchen.

"Morning," he said generally. Then he asked, "Beth, can you do something about this?" He produced a small black puppy from inside his jacket.

"Alec, it's soaking wet!" said Beth, taking the puppy. "Poor little mite. Whose is it?"

"I don't know," said Alec, as Beth began to rub the puppy dry on the kitchen towel. "But whoever it is didn't want it. One of our tractor drivers was biking past Benningham Pond this morning, and he saw the pup struggling in the water. Someone had tied its hind legs together and chucked it in."

"Oh, no!" gasped Kate.

Peter had come in unnoticed. He kicked his boots off, and Kate poured him a cup of tea. "One for you, Alec?" she said.

"Please. That's wicked, that is," he went on, frowning at the puppy. "People should take them down to the vet if they don't want them."

"I don't like killing things," Peter agreed, "but I'd shoot it rather than do that. We'll want a dog, Beth."

"We'll see," said Beth. The puppy was shivering violently. "Warm some milk, Kate, and I'll put a spot of glucose in it."

"Is that a dog or a bitch?" asked Peter.

"Bitch," said Beth. "Make a change."

The puppy lapped its warm milk energetically, then looked up with small bright eyes. It licked its nose with a surprisingly pink tongue. Beth produced a cardboard box and a bit of old blanket and installed the puppy in front of the Aga. In no time it was fast asleep.

"Goodness," said Kate. "I hadn't thought– Alec, you don't know my father, do you? He's just come from Australia!"

"So I heard," said Alec, shaking hands with Kate's father.

"I met Tom in the Fox last night," Peter explained.

"I'm glad you came," said Alec. "That's marvelous for Kate." Then he turned to Kate and said, "Where's this baby then? Let's have a look at him."

"He's fast asleep upstairs," said Kate. "He's had his early feeding, and I'll give him his bath later."

"Then I'll tiptoe up and peep in the crib," said Alec. "OK?"

Kate laughed. "OK," she said. Leading the way upstairs, she remembered how Laurie was the one who had followed her a few weeks ago. She thought of his unwelcome approach in the bedroom and felt glad that Alec was not like that. There was something completely trustworthy about Alec. He gave her a warm, secure feeling of being cared for. She opened the bedroom door.

The baby was awake. He had kicked off his blanket and was lying happily on his back in the sunlight, his hands and feet feeling the air.

"Oh," breathed Alec, "isn't he super? You are clever, Kate." He leaned over the crib and offered a finger to the little clutching hand. It was taken and grasped firmly. "He's strong, too. I told you you'd have a boy. What's his name?"

"Thomas Rowley. I hope your father won't mind."

"He'll be thrilled," said Alec. "Look, I'm awfully sorry I didn't come and see you in hospital. I would have done, but we've been combining until dark, and we're a man short. I couldn't leave Dad to it."

"No, of course not. I didn't expect you to come, anyway."

"Why not?"

"Well, after that stupid nurse taking you for my husband, it might have been a bit—"

"Don't be daft. Good Lord, you *know* I wouldn't mind."

Kate felt confused. Perhaps she did know, really. "What about some breakfast?" she suggested. "Have you had any yet?"

"I'd love some. I didn't stop because of the pup. Can we take the lad downstairs? He'll cry if I take my finger away."

"No, he won't."

Alec gently withdrew his finger from the baby's grasp, but Thomas Rowley continued to wave his hands about without complaint.

"There you are," said Kate triumphantly.

On the way downstairs she remembered Tessa's invitation.

"Oh, Alec, you know Tessa?"

"And Sophia Jane. Yes?"

"She's asked us to go and have a meal with them on Tuesday. She especially asked you—I think she's matchmaking or something—but you'll still be combining, won't you?"

They were in the kitchen now.

"It is a bit difficult," Alec admitted. "Mike broke his arm, you see, silly mutt. Motorbike accident. And we need two to each combine—"

"What's the matter?" asked Kate's father. When Alec explained, he spread his hands derisively. "What *are* you fussing about? I can do anything you can, that's for sure. Tell your dad I'll be over on Tuesday." He looked at Alec consideringly. "Last time I saw you,

you must have been about eight. And you were the skinniest matchstick of a kid that ever walked."

Alec grinned affably, quite unruffled.

"I was a late developer," he said.

17

"It's quite like old times," said Kate as the Land-Rover roared along the lane that led to Hadham. "When you used to take me to the prenatal clinic. It's much nicer having the baby with us in his car bed. I'd had enough of being pregnant by the time he was born."

"I expect you were sick of wearing maternity clothes, too," said Alec. "You look super in that dress."

"Thank you," said Kate. To cheer herself up in the days when she had been making smocks and stretchy-top trousers, she had bought some smoky-brown crepe and had made it into a simple, long-skirted dress with a row of tiny pearl buttons down the front. Working the buttonholes had taken hours, but now that she could wear the dress she knew that the effort had been well worthwhile.

The evening light had the golden, intoxicating luminosity peculiar to Suffolk, bathing stubble fields and still-standing wheat in a warm, clear glow. Kate sighed. "Isn't it beautiful?" she said. "I think I'll always come back to Suffolk."

"You're not going to London after all, are you?" asked Alec, sounding outraged. "I thought you'd finished with that chap."

"So I have," Kate assured him. Suddenly she knew that Alec would not approve of the decision she had made. But it was her life, after all. "I'm going farther than London," she said. "Dad asked me to go back to Australia with him. He married again, you see. I've got three brothers out there that I've never seen. So it's a home to go to, in a way, and it solves all the problems of what I'd do here. He asked me on Sunday, just before you came with the puppy, and I said I'd think it over. But I told him today that I'd go. So he's going to ring the travel agent tomorrow and see if there's a seat on his flight. If not, he'll change it so that we can go together."

Alec had not attempted to interrupt her long recital. He seemed stunned. "Australia," he said, "My God."

"You see, Beth's going to sell the farm before long," Kate explained. "There'd be nowhere for me to live. I'd be back at square one. The thought of going to Australia makes me feel a bit scared, especially going to a family I've never met, but I've got to do *something.*"

"The whole thing's mad," protested Alec. "You haven't seen or heard of your father since you were quite a small kid, so he can't have cared much about you. And yet the minute he turns up you're prepared to go off to the other side of the world with him like waltzing bloody Matilda."

"It does seem crazy," Kate admitted. "But it's so lovely to see him again. And in a way I feel I ought to make up for what happened. You see—" she hesitated, then went on—"he told me all about it the other night. He wrote again and again from Australia, but Mum never answered any letters, and when we moved to Finchley he didn't even know our own new address."

"He could have got it from Beth."

"He did. And you know what Mum did? She sent his letter back all torn into little bits. Wasn't it awful?"

"Good Lord," said Alec, "she sounds a tough lady."

Kate nodded. "I love Mum," she said sadly. "She's got such a sense of style and such big ideas. If she'd really made it as an actress, she'd have been all right. But she didn't, you see. She gets a good bit of work and lives on it OK, but she's disappointed. She'd always dreamed of the big time."

"You don't get to the top by treating people badly," said Alec.

"I know. But you can't tell her. And she's awfully kind in lots of ways. She used to buy me super things when I was a kid, when she'd been paid for a job."

There was a pause. Then Alec said morosely, "I'd booked you a driving test. September the fifteenth. I suppose I'd better cancel it."

"Oh, *Alec*. What a nice thing to do! But I'll have to sell the Traveller, anyway. Laurie wants his money back."

"He *what*?"

"Well, I knew it wasn't a gift, not really. I was going to ask you about the car, but when Dad got to hear about it he said he'd deal with it straight away, bless him. So there's no desperate hurry."

Alec thumped a clenched fist against the Land-Rover's steering wheel, looking murderous. "I'd like to—" he began.

"I'm sure you would!" said Kate with a grin. "Poor old Laurie wouldn't stand a chance. The trouble is, though, if I hadn't got a car I couldn't get a job in Hadham as I'd hoped."

Alec looked at her. "You wanted to stay then? You thought you'd work in Hadham and stay at the farm?"

"Yes, I did," Kate admitted. "But it just wasn't possible. So when Dad asked me to go back with him, I simply had to say yes or no. And I couldn't see what to do if I said no, so I said yes."

"Just like that."

"Just like that," Kate agreed. "But I'm sorry, in a way."

They had reached the outskirts of Hadham, and there were bungalows with neat gardens either side of the road. The color was draining from the sky.

"What's this woman's house called?" asked Alec. He sounded as if he had lost interest in the whole out-ing. Kate glanced at him nervously, but his face told her nothing.

"Gleanings," she said. She consulted Tessa's directions and added, "You turn left at the church into Ashdown Road, and it's the second house on the right."

Alec swung the Land-Rover into a gravel in front of a newly built bungalow. The garden was bright with sunflowers and Michaelmas daisies and, rather oddly, sweet corn. "Self-sufficiency," muttered Alec rather disparagingly. "You go and ring the bell. I'll get the car crib out."

A smiling, fair-haired young man came to the door. "Hello," he said. "Come along in. Tessa's in the kitchen for a minute, up to the elbows in eggplants or something." Alec slammed the Land-Rover's tailgate shut, car crib in hand, and came toward them.

"Mike!" he said. "Well, blast, I didn't know it was you!"

Michael laughed. "Hello, Alec! Small world!"

Tessa appeared, looking very pretty with a white Victorian apron over her long dress. "Do you two know each other then?" she inquired.

"I should say so!" said Alec. "He's been trying to palm off his expensive out-of-date equipment on me for years!"

"Get off," retorted Michael cheerfully. "The way you drive a bargain, you've darn nearly bust the firm. What about that sheep netting?"

Tessa groaned. "We're in for an agricultural evening, I can see," she said to Kate, leading the way in to the sitting room. "Where shall we put Thomas Rowley? Is he better somewhere quiet?"

"He doesn't seem to mind," said Kate.

"Over here where the light won't dazzle him then," Tessa instructed. "That's fine. Now what about a drink?"

To Kate's relief, Alec did not mention her impending departure. He and Michael were deep in conversation about the economics of small-scale poultry keeping, leaving Tessa and Kate free to exchange the latest news about their respective offspring.

When there was a lull in the conversation, Kate went across to the car crib and, fishing under the cover, rather shyly produced the flat parcel she had secreted there. "I wanted you to have this," she said to Tessa.

Tessa undid the wrappings carefully, then gasped with pleasure. "Kate!" she said, "did you do this?" Her present was a winter landscape in grays and white and frosty blue, the sharp patterning of bare trees carefully drawn. Kate had mounted it on cigar-brown paper-covered board and was rather pleased herself with the way it looked.

"Michael, look!" cried Tessa, "Isn't this gorgeous!"

Michael was impressed. "It's very good," he said seriously. "Tessa didn't tell me you were an artist, Kate."

"I'm not," said Kate, blushing. "It's just something I started doing to pass the time away." She had not meant to create quite such a stir.

"I wish you'd do one of our farm, Kate," said Alec. "Dad would love it. So would Mum. She'd have it framed and hang it over the mantelpiece. But I suppose you won't have time."

Kate was saved from answering by Tessa, who asked, "Do you know Marigold Armitage?"

Kate shook her head.

"She's a very good agent," Tessa went on. "She sells paintings for lots of East Anglian artists, and she's a friend of mine. I must get you two together. Now I *must* go and fry the whitebait." And she bustled out to the kitchen.

Tessa was a good cook, and the existing friendship between the two men added to the success of the meal. When it was over and coffee had been served, Thomas Rowley woke up and began to cry.

"Feeding time," said Kate.

"Bring him in the kitchen and feed him there while I wash up," said Tessa. "It's nice and warm."

Settled in a comfortable chair with the sucking baby, Kate took the opportunity of telling her friend about her plans to go to Australia. "So the picture is a sort of going-away present," she ended.

"I see," said Tessa. "And what about Alec?"

"*What* about Alec?" returned Kate in some irritation. "I do wish you'd stop trying to cook up a romance between Alec and me, Tessa. He just doesn't think of me that way. Why should he?"

Tessa surveyed her friend in exasperated silence for a minute, then whisked off to the living room. Footsteps returned, but instead of Tessa Michael was the one who came in, to Kate's slight embarrassment.

"Sorry," he said. "Forgive me disturbing your privacy, but I've been sent for some ice." He was delving about in the fridge with his back turned to Kate, carefully not disturbing her as she fed the baby. "I thought there was plenty in there," he added to the frozen depths, "but she seems to think it's got warm or something."

"Don't worry about me," said Kate. "After feeding a baby in hospital where everybody is looking, you get over being embarrassed."

"I suppose you do," he said with a quick smile. "I've got used to it too, with Tessa feeding Sophia. Can I get you a drink?"

"I'd love some squash or something," said Kate. "I seem to be awfully thirsty these days."

"Tessa's the same," said Michael. "I suppose when you're feeding these guzzly babies it's understandable."

Kate laughed. He was a nice man to be a dad.

Alec drove home in silence.

"Did you enjoy yourself?" asked Kate, not sure what he was thinking.

"Yes. Super."

"She's a good cook, isn't she?"

"Very good."

"Fancy you and Michael knowing each other."

"M'm."

Kate gave up trying. Alec drove on for a while and then suddenly he pulled off the road, hauled on the hand brake, and switched the engine off.

"What's the matter?" asked Kate, alarmed.

"Nothing." He turned to face her, one hand still gripping the steering wheel. The moon was bright, and she could see his face clearly. He looked very worried.

"Kate. I've got to ask you something."

"What?"

"Don't go to Australia."

"But why? Look, you know how things are, Alec. When Beth—"

"Oh, do shut up a minute," he said testily. "You keep talking all the time."

"Sorry." She was offended.

"No, I didn't mean to be rude, but this is so difficult." Alec ran his hand through his mop of curly hair. "I wouldn't have said anything, you see, only you going to blasted Australia, I've got to. At least, she said I'd got to."

"Who did?"

"Your friend Tessa. Sent Mike out for ice. Don't know why he went. She didn't need any ice."

"Alec," said Kate, puzzled, "have I done something

to upset you? Didn't you want to come to Tessa's tonight? Because if—"

"No, of *course* you haven't!" shouted Alec. "I just want to marry you, that's all! I know you won't and it's stupid to ask and you'll laugh, but you can't go off to bloody Australia without me even mentioning it."

"Alec. Oh, Alec." Kate put both hands to her face, not sure whether to laugh or cry. "I never thought, I didn't know—"

"Of course you didn't," said Alec gloomily. "That's why I wasn't going to ask you. Not yet, anyway."

"I always thought you had some girl friend tucked away," said Kate. "Some clever, beautiful girl who belonged to the Young Farmers' Club."

"Sick of girl friends," said Alec. "I told you, a wife is something to choose carefully."

Kate shook her head slowly. If only she had known. "It's too late," she said, numb with the pity of it all. "I can't go back on my word now. I've only just met my father again after all these years. I can't let him down."

Alec stretched his arms straight against the steering wheel and gave a gusty sigh. "OK," he said, "Shouldn't have asked." Even now he refused self-pity, accepting the inevitable with a farmer's philosophic toughness. But Kate could see in the moonlight that his mouth was set in a hard, unhappy line.

"If only I'd known," she said. But the roar of the

Land-Rover's engine drowned her voice as Alec started down the lane again. Miserably she stared out across the moonlit fields that could have been the setting to her home. The familiar lane unfolded in the headlights until they came to the track that led to Willow Farm. A square of orange light glowed in the shadowy outline of the house. "Beth's still up," she said, trying to make conversation. "Talking to Dad, I expect."

Alec made no reply. He stopped the Land-Rover in the yard and said, "I won't come in." But he switched off the engine and the headlights, and the quiet darkness flooded in. Kate stared at the orange window. A wild conviction was growing in her mind, pushing out all doubts. This was where she belonged. She turned to Alec.

"Perhaps Dad *wouldn't* mind," she said.

"Oh, Kate." Alec gathered her into his arms. "Of course he wouldn't mind." And then, very gently, he kissed her.

"I thought you were just being kind," said Kate huskily.

"Well, I wasn't," said Alec.

"I'm glad."

They kissed each other for a long time, although it seemed no time at all after the months of being alone.

"They'll be wondering what's happened to us," said Alec.

"Yes," said Kate. Neither of them moved.

"You will marry me, won't you?" said Alec.

"Yes," said Kate, kissing him again. Then she said, "Alec—"

"What?"

"Are you *sure* you don't mind about the baby?"

"You silly thing," said Alec gently, "of course I'm sure. Blast, girl," he added, dropping into Suffolk, "I got two for the price of one, ha'n't I?"

Kate laughed. "Isn't it funny," she said, "I called him Thomas so he wouldn't be another Rowley Carling, and now he's going to be another Tom Fairchild!"

"Rowley Fairchild," said Alec.

"Rowley Fairchild," Kate repeated. "What a beautiful name. Oh, Alec, I can't believe it's happening. Where shall we live?"

"Right here, most likely," said Alec. He smiled at Kate's astonished face. "Beth always thought it was the land my dad was interested in, but it was the house. He said to me years ago, 'You find yourself a wife, bor, that'll make a good place to set up.' "

Kate shook her head. "It can't be true," she said. "It's too perfect. There must be a snag somewhere."

"Oh, there is," said Alec, grinning. "It's me! You don't know what you've let yourself in for."

"I'll risk it," said Kate. "I've been so silly," she added. "Too broody to see what was happening. I always thought about you, though, right from that first morning in the kitchen. You were wearing a brown-colored sweater with leather patches on the elbows.'

"And you were wearing jeans and a red shirt with a long black cardigan."

"So I was. Oh, Alec!"

Behind them the baby stirred in the car crib and uttered a spluttering cry.

"Hungry again," said Kate.

"All right, Rowley Fairchild," said Alec over his shoulder. "You win." He jumped out and ran around to the tailgate, and as Kate went to help him lift the car crib out, light suddenly flooded across the yard. In a moment Beth came out of the house with Kate's father behind her.

"*There* you are," said Beth. "We were wondering where you'd got to."

"Oh, Beth, we've got something marvelous to tell you!" said Kate, and she and Alec approached the house with the car crib between them.

Beth smiled. "Come along in," she said, as she had done on that first bitter night when Kate had come to Willow Farm.

"We can't both get through the door together," said Alec. "Give me the crib."

Standing aside to let him go in, Kate looked up at the huge moon that hung above the fields, shining across the buildings and yard with its dreamlike, colorless light. But it wasn't a dream. It was real. She turned and followed Alec into the warm glow of the house.

About the Author

Alison Prince studied to be an artist at the Slade School and Goldsmith's College in England. She first earned her living as a teacher, occasionally selling paintings and etchings. After her marriage and the birth of three children, she turned to writing. She has contributed articles to the *Times Educational Supplement* and collaborated on a story that became the basis for a television series. She has also written several books for younger children. Her first novel for young adults, *The Doubting Kind*, was published in the United States in 1977.